SAGE BRUSH AND SIX-GUNS

Borgo Press Books by CHARLES BECKMAN

Honky-Tonk Girl: A Crime Novel
Sage Brush and Six-Guns: A Novel of the Old West

SAGE BRUSH AND SIX-GUNS

A NOVEL OF THE OLD WEST

CHARLES BECKMAN

THE BORGO PRESS

MMXII

SAGE BRUSH AND SIX-GUNS

FIRST BORGO PRESS EDITION

Published by Wildside Press LLC

www.wildsidebooks.com

DEDICATION

For my grandsons,

Jayden and Micah

Thanks also to Ron Detterman for his
assistance in scanning and formatting the
original copy of this book.

CONTENTS

CHAPTER ONE

Old Thirty-Thirty Martinue was a good man in the Texas brush country when he kept away from women. But regularly every spring the urge got into his blood and he went into town to get the bristles scraped off his jaws and have himself doused with lilac water. Then he tanked up on Joe Gideon barrel whisky and went courting.

These were the times that hell broke loose in Cherokee Flats and the clerk in the country record office cussed and got drunk himself. For when Thirty-Thirty fell in love, he was a man of great chivalry and brave deeds. He proclaimed to the world his devotion and undying love to his new-found lady by making her initial his official cattle brand, causing no end of confusion in the county records, not to mention discomfort to his stock.

So when Thirty-Thirty banged out of the Hard Luck saloon that day, roaring full of Joe Gideon, the county clerk sighed and sharpened a fresh pencil, and Hank Springer, the town blacksmith, began heating up his branding-iron stock.

Thirty-Thirty set his unsteady course first for the

tattoo professor who had put up his tent along with the other scattered tents, frame shacks, lean-tos, dugouts, and wickiups that constituted the business district of the trail town settlement of Cherokee Flats. All the way down the rutted street he bawled like a freshly branded calf that a woman was a guileful creature not to be trusted under any circumstances. He burst into the tattoo tent, threw a fistful of gold pieces in the face of the frightened professor, and ordered him to get that gol-danged purple Circle B—his current brand—off his chest or face the consequences. There was little doubt what the "consequences" were. They were contained in the cylinders of the forty-five he held menacingly in one hoary fist.

The professor did the best he could, getting himself knocked flat when he first pricked Thirty-Thirty's hide with his needle and being hauled back by the scruff of his neck when he bolted out of the tent.

The now despised Circle B (named in honor of Bessie) finally off his own hide, Thirty-Thirty took another snort out of a bottle the professor kept on hand, hiked up his belt, and aimed his course at the county clerk's shack to have the brand legally removed from his stock.

It was halfway to that point that he encountered Sheriff Ben Fry. The lawman was coming from the Red Lantern saloon and he looked as mad as Thirty-Thirty.

"Hey, Thirty-Thirty, hold up a minute!" he called.

The old brush popper spun around, his blue eyes glittering under a hedge of grey eyebrows. "Ain't got time for jawin', Ben," he snapped. "Got business to tend to."

He started on his course again, but Fry caught up with him and grabbed his belt. "Danged right you got business to tend to," he said, "but it ain't in the direction you're headed!"

Thirty-Thirty turned again. This time his jutting hedge of brows was lowered ominously. "Don't you go rilin' me," he warned the sheriff.

Fry ignored the threat. "This time your horsin' around has got you in trouble, Thirty-Thirty," he said.

The old cattleman's eyes narrowed. "What the Sam Hill are you talkin' about?" he asked cautiously.

"You know danged well what the Sam Hill I'm talkin' about. I'm talkin' about a woman from San Antonio named Bessie Martinue, that's what I'm the Sam Hill talkin' about."

"Now you listen to me, Ben——"

The sheriff out shouted him. "No, you listen to me! I know the whole story, so it ain't no use in you gettin' off on one of your long-winded lies, Thirty-Thirty. I got it right from her lips. When you went on that binge last spring, you wound up in San-tone. You met Bessie at a fandango down on Haymarket Plaza. You up an' married her and went on raisin' hell for three days before you deserted her an' come back here to your ranch——"

"Now hold on right there, Ben!" Thirty-Thirty said indignantly. "I never deserted no lawfully deservin' wife of mine! That Bessie is a lyin' gold-digger, that's what she is. Just a lyin' gold-digger. I'll admit we got together up in San-tone last spring and maybe I did go with her to a preacher to make it legal. But when I wanted her to come back to my ranch, which I'd just decided to rename the Circle B in her honor—in her honor, mind ye—would she come? No sir! I offered to take her back so's she could do the cookin' an' sewin' and chores like a man's wife's supposed to do an' she says she'll join me later. Later, huh! I keep a-waitin' an' goin' down to meet every stage that come in from Santone for the next month. Ain't no hide or hair of Bessie on nary one of 'em. Then I finally got this letter from her. She says she thought it over an' decided she ain't cut out to be no ranch wife and to forget the whole thing."

Thirty-Thirty's mustache drooped with injured pride. "Ain't that a low-down trick to play on a man, Ben? And then what's that brazen hussy got the sass to do but all of a sudden show up here in Cherokee Flats nine months later, demandin' part interest in my ranch. She got in town yesterday and don't hardly drop her bags down from the stagecoach before she sent word by Meskin Lupe out to my ranch that she's comin' to claim half of my spread. Well, she ain't gittin' it! Furthermore, I ain't even gonna see her. Further more, I ain't gonna support her! Not one cent. Now you go put me in jail, Ben. Go on, put me! I don't care what she—"

"You don't have to support her, if that's what you're bawling about," Ben Fry cut in wearily. "She's dead."

There was a moment of stunned silence. Across the street, at a mesquite hitch rail, a horse whinnied.

"Huh?"

"I said she's dead," Fry said.

Thirty-Thirty's jaw dropped. His eyes bulged. Finally he said gently, "Aw, what'd she go and do that for?"

"I reckon because she was so pizened up, carryin' any young'un of yours."

Again there was a stricken silence. Then Thirty-Thirty asked suspiciously, his eyes still bugged out, "What young'un?"

"Yores," Ben Fry said. "She birthed a little boy and up and died, just like that. It happened about an hour ago over to the Red Lantern saloon. The Mexican woman, Lolita Flóres, was midwifin' for her."

Thirty-Thirty's bleary blue eyes bulged even more. His Adam's apple raced up and down his stringy neck as he gulped audibly. "You—you mean—" he whispered hoarsely.

"I mean," Ben Fry snapped, "you're a papa. You went and got yourself a son, and by Harry, you're gonna support that kid, Thirty-Thirty! I ain't allowin' no babies layin' around Cherokee Flats to become public charges of this township while their papa is strong, able, an' available."

All the wind out of his sails now, Martinue meekly followed the sheriff over to the Red Lantern saloon, a rough frame shed housing a dirt floor and a "bar" that consisted of two planks laid across upended whisky kegs. The dead woman was in the back on a cot, covered by an army blanket. The Mexican midwife, young and buxom, cradled the new-born baby in her arms, crooning to it softly in Spanish.

Thirty-Thirty sidled up to his son, his sombrero brim crushed in his sweating; hands. He craned his neck and focused his awe-filled eyes at the red-faced, howling mite of humanity.

"Gawd!" he breathed, then glanced at the faces ringed around him. "My son." He looked back at the kid, slowly getting used to the idea. When it had sunk in enough, he suddenly puffed out his chest and grinned. "My son. That there's my son!"

The event had suspended the poker games and the drinking in the saloon and everybody was crowded around Thirty-Thirty, staring at him and poking at the infant. "What you gonna name him, Thirty-Thirty?" someone asked.

Thirty-Thirty pulled at his mustache and scowled. "Ain't give it much thought," he admitted.

"Jesse's a nice name," a Mexican mule-skinner volunteered. "I had a cousin named Jesse. He chure wassa fine hombre. He got hung over een Torreon for stealin' a horse."

Other names were suggested and rejected. Then Thirty-Thirty's eyes fell on the roughly lettered sign over the bar. "I'll name him 'Red' after this here Red Lantern saloon where he was birthed!" the brush popper announced. "Allus wanted a son named Red, anyhow."

He gave vent to an ear-splitting whoop! "Drinks are on me, fellers!" He told the Mexican woman to give the infant all the whisky he wanted, but to cut it with some milk. Then he swaggered to the door. "Reckon I'll go down to th' record office and change my brand. From now on it'll be the Lazy R, after my son, Red."

Thirty-Thirty hired Lolita Flóres to come out to his ranch and care for the infant and he rode into the newly rechristened Lazy R ranch yard with them that evening in his buckboard just as the sun was setting behind the chaparral thicket and the doves were whirring into the tank for their evening water.

He stood up and shook his fist at the acres of dense brush stretching to the west. "I got me a son. You hear that, Josiah Zepeda? I'm gonna spread my land and build my herd. Together me an' my boy will build a cattle empire that'll make yore Boxed X look like a sheep farm! We're gonna push you right into the Rio Grande and then stand on the bank and watch you drown in it!"

And that was how Red Martinue came into the world one late fall day in Texas, born to the brush country, the saddle, and the start of a private empire.

CHAPTER TWO

That same night, far away in the hot, crowded French Quarter of New Orleans, another child was born, a girl, to the French Creole woman Adrienne Marcie. The room was near the French market, in the shadow of the St. Louis Cathedral. Under the window covered with iron grillwork was a courtyard filled with banana trees. The room itself had a faded elegance in its worn red carpet and a few pieces of heavy oak furniture. Wide cornices ran around the white plastered walls. In one corner of the room there was a flowering oleander in a green pot.

This was the sad remains of a once-luxurious house belonging to the General Marcie, Adrienne's grandfather, who had served under Napoleon. When the Little Emperor was exiled, some of his trusted friends had come to New Orleans to prepare a home for him here, but he died before the plot to slip him off the Island of St. Helena was carried out. So, among others who had worked at the plan, General Marcie remained for the rest of his life in New Orleans, banished from France.

What small wealth he had brought with him was

used up in his lifetime. The next generation of Marcies sold the house and declined to the status of common laborers. But sometimes Adrienne's mother would bring her to this street and point out the old house that once had belonged to their family and remind her that she was pure French, poor, perhaps, but nevertheless a Creole—one of the aristocracy of New Orleans, a descendant of the true sons and daughters of France.

The story and the house made a great impression on little Adrienne. It was like a fairy tale. The Marcie house had once been a castle and she was a princess, banished from it, but destined to return one day. Even after she grew up and worked as a barmaid, the legend persisted in her. The men who knew her in the bar thought she was pompous and vain for a daughter of old Henri Marcie, a ditch-digger who was always drunk and dirty.

But Adrienne paid no attention to them. Sometimes at dusk she walked down to Jackson Square and over to the narrow street where the Marcie house was. Her biggest ambition was to buy the house someday. But then it was turned into a rooming house and the closest she ever came to her dream was when she rented a room in the house.

Generally, she hated the men who came to the saloon. They tried to pinch her, and made coarse remarks and they reminded her of her drunken father. But Bruce was different. He was a young medical student and he came from a plantation family that owned land, cotton and slaves in Louisiana. He was from the aristocracy of the old South and that made a real impression on Adrienne. It wasn't until later that she realized he was also weak. And then it was too late.

This night, the flickering candlelight played on the perspiring face of pretty Adrienne Marcie. Pain turned the beauty into contorted grimaces. Then, at last, a look of exhausted peace came to her face. Her eyelids fluttered. She looked up at the young man who was attending her, the father of her child. "Bruce," she whispered, "you are so frightened. Your hands tremble. Is it a boy or a girl?" Adrienne had been seven years old before she learned a word of English and she still spoke with a French accent.

Bruce Harrell wiped his pale face, a handsome, slender face with long sideburns correctly measured to the style of the day. The sleeves of his ruffled white shirt were rolled up. There was a heavy gold chain across his vest. His coat and hat were on a chair where he'd thrown them when he came in.

"A girl, Adrienne," he said shakily. "A beautiful girl." He laid the infant in its mother's arms. Then he sank into a chair, holding his face in his hands. "Frightened? Yes, I am frightened, Adrienne. We have a child— If my parents find out about you—about us, they'll stop my allowance. I'll never be able to finish school—"

There was an even greater fear in him that he didn't put into words. If the authorities found that he had practiced tonight without a license, he would be expelled from school.

Adrienne smiled at him with veiled contempt in

her flashing black eyes. "Afraid. Always afraid! You are like a little boy!" Then she pressed her lips to the forehead of her daughter. "And you, my sweet one," she whispered in French, "I will name you Celeste. You will never be afraid of anything. You will have weapons to fight with in this world of weak men. Soft, entrancing weapons with little steel claws hidden in them. I will teach you how to use those weapons, little one, so that you do not become what your mother is, a barmaid, depending on the shaky honor of a weak-livered, spoiled brat—"

"Stop talking that infernal French!" Bruce Harrell cut in. "You know I can't understand it. Then, nervously, he darted to the door and stood against it, listening, certain he'd heard a footstep out in the hallway.

His fears materialized. A snooping landlady had been outside in the hall, an ear pressed to the door. She informed to the authorities. They found Bruce Harrell guilty of practicing medicine without a license and he was fined and expelled from school. His parents cut off his allowance and refused to see him, and now he was penniless. There was left to him but one place to go— West, where doctors were needed—so greatly needed that men didn't check into the validity of a medical diploma, which could be forged.

Bruce Harrell took Adrienne and little Celeste with him into the new, dangerous world. They crossed the prairie in a schooner, the child, in her mother's arms, unaware of the destiny that was going to bring her, twenty-one years later, to Cherokee Flats and to Red

Martinue and to the brush country empire known as the Lazy R ranch.

CHAPTER THREE

Thirty-Thirty Martinue raised his son to know well the secrets of the brush country, the ways of the saddle, and the windings of the long cattle trails north.

Content before to hold together a mangy herd of scrub longhorns that paid for his chuck, enough chewing tobacco, and an annual spring romance, Thirty-Thirty was filled now with a driving ambition. He wanted land, a vast spread of land, filled with cattle. He wanted to extend the Lazy R boundaries to the far reaches of the brush country.

Red grew in stature and strength, nurtured first on goat's milk and then on *frijole* beans and beef. Before he could walk he had learned the feel of saddle leather.

"The monte's no place for a weakling," Thirty-Thirty often muttered to the growing boy. "It's good country, where a man can stay as free as he's strong. But first he's got to be strong or he won't stay at all. That there brush is like a catamount with claws, jest waitin' to scratch your eyes out. You got to learn to outsmart it an' outride it an' then you got it licked."

Before he was ten, Red knew the ways of the brush poppers, the lanky, bearded men who fought the brush for their cattle. He had a pair of *chaparajos* and *tapaderos* to protect his feet and legs from the stabbing thorns of the mesquite, retama, junco, and cactus. Thirty-Thirty taught him how to plow into the brush head-on, riding all over his horse, under first one side, then the other, dodging the flying limbs and thorns that stabbed at his face and eyes while he ran down a wild-eyed longhorn *ladino* and roped him with his short, brush-style rawhide *reata*. At night he came in, stiff and sore, bruised by limbs and stabbed by thorns, and Thirty-Thirty made poultices of prickly pear and kerosene to ease the soreness and draw out the thorns.

The monte was filled with game—black bear, antelope, white-tailed deer, and javalina hogs. Every creek bottom had its wild turkeys, and there were white-winged doves and coveys of quail hunting berries from the agrito bushes. When he had time, Red hunted game to supplement the steady Lazy R diet of corn bread, molasses, sowbelly, *frijole* beans, and chicory coffee.

As Red grew older the bad blood between the ranch to the west, the Boxed X, and the Lazy R, grew worse. The Boxed X was by far the biggest ranch in the southwest corner of Texas. It sprawled north from Brownsville, along the Rio Grande, spreading its boundaries off to include the best water holes and grazing areas. And Josiah Zepeda, the owner, was by far the richest man in that part of the state. Besides the ranch, he owned most of Cherokee Flats, including the only bank in the town, and two steamboats that brought freight all the way up the Rio Grande from the mouth near Brownsville to Laredo, and he had investments both in Mexico and in the East.

At first Josiah Zepeda viewed Thirty-Thirty Martinue and the little herd he ran on the Lazy R with tolerance and amusement. But suddenly Thirty-Thirty had ceased to be a harmless old brush rat. He hired some Mexican riders who were as handy with a forty-five as they were with a *reata*. Zepeda, who for years had adjusted the boundaries of his ranch to his own pleasure, suddenly found he had run against a wall at the southeast, where he fringed the little Lazy R. He was further disturbed because Thirty-Thirty's Mexican riders, who couldn't read English, also couldn't seem to read cattle brands.

That was Zepeda's contention. Thirty-Thirty swore he never touched a head bearing another man's brand. But, he pointed out, if he ran into a herd of brush cattle without brands, he had as much right to them as Zepeda or the President of the United States, and that they happened to be roaming on Boxed X land had nothing to do with it. In this practice Thirty-Thirty was simply following a Texas custom of the times. Technically, much of Texas was open range, anyway; and moreover, Thirty-Thirty might have asked Josiah Zepeda where he had started his herds. This would have been an embarrassing question for Zepeda, since, like any respectable, wealthy Texas cattleman, he had stolen the bulk of his herd to begin with.

But it was not so much a question of ethics as it was of survival. As long as the Lazy R amounted to no more than a modest spread, apologetically running a few head, and showing no ambition toward expansion, Zepeda didn't care if Thirty-Thirty's riders did help themselves to a few *ladinos* roaming through his brush. After all, just whom a wild, unbranded longhorn belonged to was a debatable question.

But when the change came over Thirty-Thirty, when he hired the *vaqueros*, out of Chihuahua, when the *ladinos* began pouring into his corrals instead of straggling in occasionally, and when the Boxed X's boundaries, which had been slowly creeping eastward for years, suddenly halted, then began creeping back—then the Lazy R changed from a thorn in Josiah Zepeda's side to a serious threat.

Zepeda was not a stupid man. He was a far-seeing man. He measured the things now happening against the future and what he saw made him uncomfortable. The southwest corner of Texas, although the size of a half-dozen eastern states, didn't cover enough land to support two men as ambitious and powerful as he.

To Zepeda, range war was an ugly thing and he shied away from the thought of it. But when he rode through his brush country and looked uncomfortably toward the southeast, something prickled up his spine. A glimpse of the future flitted across his mind and he couldn't see anything but trouble in store.

The looming fight between the Boxed X and the Lazy R didn't take on a personal aspect for Red Martinue until he was fifteen years old.

Since he was eight, Red had been forced to supplement his range education with a certain amount of book learning, something he considered a complete waste of time. Rain or shine, hot or cold, he had to saddle up his horse every morning at six-thirty and ride to the schoolhouse in Cherokee Flats. Thirty-Thirty had impressed on him, with a length of harness strap, his determination that the future owner of the Lazy R would be able to read and figure as well as he knew how to lasso.

It was a typical country school of the day, one big room, with grades ranging from one to eight, and pupils from six to sixteen. Attending the school along with Red was Duncan Zepeda, the son of Josiah Zepeda. Duncan, two years older than Red, hung around with the older boys, and during the years when the animosity between the Boxed X and the Lazy R was just forming, he paid little attention to Red. But in the past year Duncan had heard his father swearing about the practices of the Lazy R riders more and more and he'd begun to look on Red with a natural hostility.

The real trouble between them broke out on Red's fourteenth birthday. That was the day of the big spelling match. For weeks Red had been anticipating the day with both hope and dread. That morning, he crawled out of his bunk at five instead of the usual six. Thirty-Thirty was still snoring in his bunk, and in another bedroom Lolita Flóres, Red's *mamacita* since the day of his birth, was still sleeping, too.

Red went out on the back porch and washed his face in a basin of icy water. He was at the tall, skinny state that comes to boys of his age, and his thin body shivered in the frosty early morning air. He pulled on his boots, went out to the corral and saddled up the little pinto he'd been riding since he was twelve, then set out toward Cherokee Flats. He hadn't closed his eyes all night, and the way his stomach was all twisted in knots told him he couldn't eat any breakfast. For this was to be the most gol-danged, ring-tailed, wing-hootin' spelling match the professor had ever put on at their school.

The professor had gone up to Laredo a month ago, when the Zepeda steamboat docked after its run up the river from Brownsville. He'd shopped among the wares on board and bought a pocket knife and a bolt of cloth.

This wasn't just any ordinary pocket knife or any ordinary bolt of cloth. The knife had been made in a very fine steel factory in Germany. It was part of a shipment to New Orleans and then to Brownsville. The handle was a bone smoothed and polished to a dull finish that felt like silk. It had a master blade shaped like a Bowie and fully six inches long. And there was a small blade for paring, and a third blade in the shape of a long, pointed awl.

It was by far the most beautiful knife that Red had ever laid his eyes on. No mail-order catalogue had ever featured anything like this German-made beauty. And the bolt of dress cloth was a very fine fabric shipped all the way from Scotland. Both the knife and the bolt of cloth had been on display at the front of the class for a month, ever since the professor had announced the awesome news that they would be awarded as prizes to the winners of the big spelling bee. The best boy speller in the class was to receive the knife, and the bolt of cloth was to go to the girl winner.

The next month had been sheer torture. Every morning before the professor rapped on his desk for order, the girls clustered around the fine Scotch-plaid cloth, and the boys around the knife. There wasn't a girl present who wouldn't have scratched out the eyes of all her rivals for a dress made out of that cloth. And the boys all wished desperately that they could fight with bare fists for that wonderful knife, instead of having to go through the torture of spelling for it.

Red suffered torment that month. He was a better-than-average speller, but every time he looked at the coveted prize, pangs of inadequacy haunted him. He studied his speller until his eyes throbbed and he'd committed every word in it to memory. He haunted his Pa's *vaqueros* for good-luck pieces and each one contributed a favorite talisman that had proven itself in countless games of poker. Red's pockets bulged with lodestones, rabbit's feet, lion's teeth, and shark bones.

And now it was the fateful day.

Red stood along the wall with the others, such a quivering, trembling wreck that when the words came his way, he could barely whisper the letters.

The professor plodded up and down before the row

of sweating boys, hands clasped under the tails of his frock coat, glaring at them over the gold rims of his glasses.

"Now, R-R-Red," the professor said in his deep German accent, rolling his Rs like a base drum, "your negst vo-r-r-rd iss 'gallant'."

Red gulped, clamped his eyes shut and whispered, "G—g—a—l—er—l—e—n—no!—a—n—t."

The words droned on. One by one the boys sank to their seats in dazed disappointment. And suddenly the miracle took place! Red looked around and he was the only one left standing. The professor was clapping him on the shoulder. Something was pressed into his sweating palm. He looked down and saw it there, the smooth, gleaming perfection of the wonderful knife he'd won.

Every other boy in the class was staring at him sullenly, enviously. But there was more than envy in the narrowed, hate-filled eyes of Duncan Zepeda.

Out in the yard during the next recess the girl winner and Red were the center of attention.

They were grudgingly congratulated. All Red's friends demanded that he pass the knife around for inspection, as if they hadn't already memorized every inch of it.

Red was standing in the center of a group of boys when Duncan Zepeda came shouldering through to stand in front of Red. He was older and bigger than the others and he had already proved that he could lick any other boy in school. The boys gave him room respectfully. He stood in front of Red with his fists on his hips, sneering.

"Think you're pretty smart, winnin' that knife, don't you?"

Red had had his share of fights along with other boys who went to school, but he'd never faced up to anybody as big as Duncan Zepeda. His mouth suddenly went dry.

There was the electric feeling that boys in a school yard sense the instant a fight is about to start. In a flash they had ringed around Duncan and Red.

Red didn't answer. He just stood spraddle-legged, the knife clenched in his hand.

Duncan looked down at the prize knife and snickered. "Lemme see that knife. It probably ain't nothin' but junk, anyway. I bet I can break the blade easy."

Red felt as though somebody had stuffed a fistful of cotton in his mouth. His knees began quivering. But he tightened his grip on the knife and thrust it in his pocket, keeping his fist around it.

Duncan started looking meaner. He had a pug nose and a rash of freckles. He was built heavy and square like his father. His shirttail was hanging out and he smelled strong of perspiration. "I said, gimme the knife."

Red's vocal chords were paralyzed. All he could do was shake his head and cling desperately to the knife in his pocket.

Duncan's hand suddenly shot out. He pushed Red's shoulder hard with his fingers and the lighter boy took a step backward. Duncan moved closer, thrusting his face to within inches of Red's. "Your old man's a stinkin', dirty cattle thief," he said distinctly. "He's stealin' my pa's cattle. You're nothin' but the son of a dirty, stinkin' cattle thief!"

A murmur ran through the crowd of boys. They edged closer, eager for the fight to begin. "Hit him, Red," a boy yelled.

"Yeah, what's th' matter, you gonna let him get away callin' you that, Red?"

"You yella, Red?"

"Yella!"

Duncan gave Red another push. The boys crowded closer in a dusty, squirming knot, jeering and taunting Red Martinue because he was taking the insults and wasn't fighting back.

There were tears of rage and fear in Red's eyes, blinding him. He was shaking all over. How was he going to hit the sneering face before him if his muscles had turned into jelly?

Suddenly a boy yelped, "Here comes the professor!"

In a flash the knot dissolved, boys scattering in all directions.

Duncan jammed his face close to Red, spitting through his teeth, "I'll be waitin' for you on the way home after school, bastard!" Then he walked off.

The rest of the day was a nightmare. Red sat behind his desk in a daze. He had a fever. His head throbbed and his eyes felt swollen and hot. His stomach had a sick, queasy feeling.

He was scared for the first time in his life. He'd never been afraid of wild horses, of snakes that infested the brush, of the wild longhorns he helped his pa round up. But now he knew he was going to get a beating this afternoon. Nothing could save him. Duncan was going to smash his face and kick him and beat him to a pulp. And all he could do was sit here and think how terrible it was going to be.

School let out at four o'clock. He moved slowly, saddling his horse. The schoolyard was completely deserted by the time he got through. He swung into the saddle and clasped the reins in his sweating hands. He started toward home. If he was lucky, he might be able to outride Duncan.

But when he got out of town, he came around a bend and there was Duncan waiting, along with a crowd of boys. They were lined across the path and there was no way for Red to escape unless he turned heel and ran.

For a second he had a wild impulse to do just that. His hand had already tightened to jerk the reins. And then a vision of Thirty-Thirty's bristling countenance shot across his mind. His pa would take his hide off in strips and run him off the ranch if he turned yellow-belly crawfish on a Zepeda.

Shakily, he got off his pinto. The late afternoon sun was slanting through the dust already stirred up in the lane. Duncan and the others came toward him. Duncan was walking with a stiff-legged swagger, his fingers already bunched up into fists.

Red's eyes had blurred with tears and he saw all this

in a haze.

Duncan came up to him. "Hello, Martinue," he sneered. "Told ya I'd be waitin' for ya. Didn't believe me, huh?"

Red kept his jaws clamped together. "I ain't gonna bawl," he thought desperately. "I ain't—I ain't gonna—"

"You come to admit your pa's stealin' my pa's cattle?" Duncan went on. "You gonna admit it? You gonna admit that Meskin woman on your place is your real maw and you ain't nothin' but the son of a cattle stealer?"

Duncan suddenly grabbed a fistful of Red's shirt. "You gimme that knife. I'm takin' it in payment for the cattle you helped steal offa our ranch, you little yellow-bellied half-Meskin. Gimme that knife—"

Red swung his fist with all his might. There was no plan or skill about it. He just doubled his fist and closed his eyes and swung as hard as he could. He was as surprised as Duncan Zepeda when it connected.

He felt his knuckles crash into something soft and yielding and a hot liquid spurt over his hand. There was a hoarse, agonized bellow. He opened his eyes and he saw Duncan Zepeda sprawled in the dust. Bright red blood was gushing out of Duncan's nose in glistening spurts. He was howling with pain and anger.

If Red had followed up his surprise attack, he might have become champion right on that spot. But he was so surprised and frightened that he could only stand there, frozen with horror at what he'd done to the awesome bully that ruled the Cherokee Flats school.

When Duncan saw that his attacker wasn't going to follow up the first advantage, he got to his feet. Still bawling, he grabbed Red's shirt, hooked his right leg behind Red's knee and gave a violent shove, tripping Red flat. Then he pounced on the smaller boy, slamming his fists one after the other into his victim's face.

The hard fall to the ground had knocked Red's breath out of him. Then the cruel knuckles were thudding into his ribs and face. Smarting pain from his pummeled nose brought tears gushing out of his eyes. Dimly he heard the yells of the other boys as he choked on the dust and his own blood and gagged for breath.

Duncan kept on until Red was half-unconscious. Then he kicked Red in the stomach and turned to the other boys. He was holding up the prize he'd taken from Red. Then he towered over the badly beaten loser.

"Now you admit it. Say it out loud so everybody can hear. Say your pa's a cattle thief and you're just the son of a stinkin' cattle thief!"

Duncan kicked him again. Through a mouthful of blood, Red mumbled the shameful admission.

Then his stomach suddenly heaved. He was drenched with icy sweat and he turned his head and vomited in the dust. Above him, he heard Duncan and the others laughing.

Finally, seeing that Red was too sick to talk and that they weren't going to get any more sport out of him, Duncan and the others walked back to the grove of mesquite trees, untied their horses and rode off.

Red lay in the dust for a long time, too weak and sick

to move. Flies buzzed over the dried blood on his face. Ants and tumble bugs came out of their hiding places and took up their interrupted business in the road. A grey horned frog wriggled out in the dust and sunned himself.

Finally, Red groaned and sat up. It was painful even to breathe, but in him was a pain much worse than the bruises, the painful humiliation of the beating. He sat with his head in his hands, miserable with shame. And then a terrible remembrance shot through him. Frantically he groped through his torn, blood-smeared clothes.

The knife, the beautiful, wonderful knife! It was gone!

That was the last straw. Red hadn't cried since his dog died when he was nine years old, but now he put his hands over his eyes and bawled with pain and humiliation and heartbreak, feeling sorry for himself and nursing a murderous hatred for Duncan Zepeda.

At last he dragged himself to his feet and got on his horse and rode homeward. On the way he stopped at a creek and washed off some of the dirt and blood. When he reached home, he sneaked into the house by a back door. In his room he peeled off his torn, blood-stained clothes and put on a fresh pair of Levis and a blue shirt. He wadded up the ruined clothes and hid them under the house.

That night at supper he lied to Thirty-Thirty for the first time in his life. When the *vaqueros* and Thirty-Thirty and Red gathered around the long table in the bunkhouse and Lolita started bringing in steaming platters of broiled venison and fresh, hot cornbread, Thirty-Thirty glanced at his son. Even in the smoky lamplight it was obvious by his swollen nose and the purple swelling under one eye that Red had been in a scrap.

Thirty-Thirty's pepper-gray mustache and eyebrows bristled. "You been fightin' on the schoolyard, Red?" he thundered.

The boy fingered a spoon, staring down at it. "N-nossir," he mumbled. "It—it was on the way home."

Thirty-Thirty speared himself a piece of venison. "Just don't let me catch you causin' no trouble on that schoolyard," he warned his son. Thirty-Thirty had a clear-cut rule about fighting.

It was an accepted fact that a growing boy had to have his share of fights, but Thirty-Thirty was paying the professor ten dollars a month for Red's schooling, as were the other parents of the kids at the school, and he didn't want Red disrupting any of that expensive time by causing mischief in the schoolyard. What went on after school was another matter.

After his third slab of venison Thirty-Thirty wiped his mustache and said, "Well, how did the spellin' match come out, son?"

There was a sudden hush. Red, who had been only picking at his food, began worrying his spoon again. He felt the eyes of all the *vaqueros* and *Mamacita* Lolita on him. He knew they'd all be proud if he told them he had won the match, but then they'd ask to see the knife and he'd have to admit the shameful truth, that he'd let the son of Josiah Zepeda whip the tar out of him and take the knife away. It was a humiliation that he couldn't bring himself to face. It was easier to lie about the spelling match.

"I didn't win," he mumbled. "Duncan Zepeda won it."

The disappointment was obvious in Thirty-Thirty's blue eyes. He was proud of his son's book learning and since he, himself, could sign his name only at the expense of much sweating and tongue chewing, winning the spelling match would have given him the vicarious thrill of his life. His long mustache drooped for a moment. Then he fiercely jabbed his fourth slab of venison and gruffly thundered, "Hell, don't feel bad about it, son. A man never learnt how to lasso a steer by spellin' purty yit!"

The *vaqueros'* white teeth flashed and everybody laughed to ease the feeling of disappointment in the room. Red fought to keep the tears back. He felt guilty about lying to Thirty-Thirty, but at least he'd covered up his humiliation. Losing a spelling match didn't make him any less of a man in the eyes of the riders of the Lazy R. But losing a fight to Duncan Zepeda would.

That night Red huddled in his bunk with his pillow stuffed in his mouth, afraid he'd start bawling if he began thinking about the knife again. He was filling his mind with beautiful pictures of himself knocking down and tromping Duncan Zepeda. Duncan was sniveling and begging not to be hit again. Red made him give him the knife. Then he made him say, "My pa is the biggest cattle thief in Texas and he steals horses, too."

Over and over Red played the scene and each time Duncan was more abjectly beaten. Red was starting on the fifth performance when the stranger rode into the yard outside his bedroom window. The sound of the hoof beats broke sharply into Red's thoughts and he held his breath, listening.

It was unusual for anybody to be riding into the Lazy R yard this time of night. As Red strained his ears he realized that that wasn't the only strange thing going on. It was long past eleven o'clock and his pa hadn't come to bed yet. That didn't make sense unless Thirty-Thirty was expecting this mysterious rider. But why would a man come calling this time of night?

His curiosity suddenly aflame, Red eased out of his bunk and crept barefooted down the hall toward the parlor of the rambling old ranch house. He peered around the door.

Three men were seated in the parlor. The dim light from a single lamp made their faces shadowy. One of the men was Thirty-Thirty, sitting in a hide-bottom straight chair propped against a wall, his boot heel hooked on one rung, his thumbs hooked in his gun belt, his blue eyes glittering toward the stranger. The second man was Manuel Vera, the foreman of the *vaqueros*. His full attention was on the mysterious caller.

Red's eyes followed the direction of their gazes and

he curiously examined the tall stranger sitting on the horsehair company sofa. The man was dressed in a strange kind of gray uniform. He wore cavalry boots so shined and polished that they reflected the lamp like mirrors.

He was saying to Thirty-Thirty: "We know the Union is going to blockade all the South's major ports. They're closing in on Charleston and New Orleans already and there'll be Union gunboats in the Gulf at Brownsville in a few days. The Confederacy's biggest struggle is going to be finding trade routes with England and France, because without them there'll be serious shortages in the South. That's why I'm going to ranchers like yourself, Mr. Martinue. I'm not selling patriotism alone. I'm selling you a business proposition. You can sell your cattle directly to the army through purchasing agents like myself and get a fair price. Or you can get a sizable herd together and cross the river into Mexico and drive them down to the Mexican port of Bagdad. There you can trade them for the goods that English merchantmen are bringing in—goods we need more than beef. You can bring those goods back across the border and we'll pay you double what your cattle would have brought—and pay you in gold."

Red listened with a puzzled frown. He didn't understand exactly what the man was talking about. During the past few months he'd heard some talk about a war with the North, but it had seemed remote and far away from this distant corner of Texas. But he understood well enough what Thirty-Thirty said to the man's proposition.

"Looks like we might do business, Mr. Samuel. I aim to spread this ranch out until it's second to none in this here state and I'll need gold to do it. What you think, Manuel? Reckon we can git a herd together and drive 'em down through Mexico?"

The foreman shrugged and smiled. "Eet ees Cortina's country, but we sure as hell try eef you esay, *patrón*."

"Cortina, hell!" Thirty-Thirty said, sending a stream of tobacco juice through an open window. He wiped off his mustache. "We'll take enough of your cousins along to chase that bandit clear out of Mexico! We'll start roundin' up that there herd tomorrow, Mr. Samuel."

"Good! Remember, England needs our cotton and beef and we need their manufactured goods. You can make yourself a rich man, Mr. Martinue."

A prickly ripple chased up Red's spine and he felt his heart pounding hard. There was a sudden electric feeling of excitement in the air. He had the feeling he was on the brink of the biggest adventure of his life.

What he didn't know was that this was the true beginning of Thirty-Thirty's dream of turning the Lazy R into the greatest brush country kingdom of Texas.

CHAPTER FOUR

"*Una Vez*." Manuel Vera began. "One time I was alone een the monte for mebbeso three weeks. I catch me lotsa head. But there ees theese black wan, theese Negro, that I do not catch. *Caramba*, he ees twice as beeg as any bull I never seen before. He was a beeg wan weeth horns like eso and eso—"

Red sat beside the campfire with his arms around his knees, listening spellbound to the story the Mexican foreman was telling. For two weeks now the Lazy R riders had been hitting the brush day and night, pulling together the herd Thirty-Thirty would take into Mexico. To his unbounded joy, Red had been allowed to chuck school and join in the roundup of brush mavericks.

He worked right alongside the *vaqueros*. They knew every thorn of the big thicket and they loved the hard, dangerous work. And at night they liked best to sit around the campfire in a clearing in the monte and play the guitar and mend harnesses, plait ropes, spin yarns.

And of all the storytellers Manuel Vera was the best. When he told a story it was more than a thing of words. He hopped about and he lay on the ground and he crawled on his belly and he waved his arms.

When describing a wild animal, he got on his hands and knees and made fierce grimaces, and when a character in his tale was performing an unbelievable feat of roping, his own hand spun an invisible *reata* in the air.

When his story about the black bull was finished, he wiped his perspiring face, catching his breath. Then he jumped up. "*Bueno*, Rojo, now we go een the brush and show thees *cabrones* how to catch cows!"

For weeks Red had been badgering Manuel to take him on one of his night hunts. Manuel was filled with tricks for outsmarting the wily brush longhorns; he always caught from ten to thirty head in a single night. But he kept his methods secret, refusing to let any other *vaqueros* accompany him. But he'd finally agreed to take Red—Rojo as he called him in Spanish—along tonight after first swearing him to secrecy on a dark oath.

Red's fingers were clumsy with excitement as he saddled his pinto.

The other *vaqueros* lounging around the fire called out good-natured taunts:

"Watch out you don' get lost weeth that Manuel!"

"*Sí*, he only takes you to show heem the way back home, Rojo."

"That Manuel ees blind een the dark. You weel fall een the Rio Grande an' drown eef you follow heem, Rojo!"

Manuel swung on his horse and called down to them that they sprang from crippled pigs on their maternal side and stupid donkeys on their paternal side.

Red gave the latigo strap on his saddle a final tug, climbed onto his mount and followed the foreman into the black wall of the monte that loomed just beyond the campfire. Of all the brush country of Texas, this section of open range that the Boxed X claimed for their cattle was the wildest.

It was bad enough during the day when the dusty, overpowering heat, the dense thickets of dagger-sharp thorns, the scarcity of water and the heavy population of rattlesnakes made it worse than a deserted corner of hell. But at night there was a blackness, a smothering stillness that made it even worse.

But to Red there was nothing strange or terrifying about the brush. His eyes, accustomed to the dark, picked out the wild desert beauty of cactus flowers. The devil's-head, the nopal, varicolored with its waxy flowers and studded with red and purple prickly-pear apples—the tasajillo, and the pitahaya. Here and there was the hardy Spanish dagger sending its flower stalk high above the scrubbier brush. And there were the golden balls of the huisache tree and the lacy retama tree blossoms showering the trail with gold. From these trees came a heavy, sweet perfume that hung in the still air.

He followed Manuel through the brush for two hours, ducking and dodging the ferociously spiked limbs almost instinctively. Then the foreman stopped his horse. "Now we walk," he whispered.

Red tied his pinto to a mesquite and followed on foot. After fifteen minutes Manuel stopped again, wiping his brow with his bandana.

"*Amigo*, I tell you sometheeng most of these dumb cowhands don' know. The cows een theese brush, they smell a man better than a wild lion does. Now we feex meester cow so he don' catch our scent. The body of a man, just een hees own hide, don't geeve off the scent like the clothes he has sweat een."

Manuel stripped off all his clothes and Red followed suit. The foreman scooped out a hole in the sandy soil and buried them. Then he said, "Now we feex eet so we smell like meester cow himself!"

He hunted around until he found a pile of half-dry cow manure beside the trail and he rubbed a handful of this with some dirt in his hair and all over his body. Red did the same.

Manuel sniffed the air and proclaimed them both indistinguishable from a cow.

Satisfied, he advanced farther into the brush for two hundred yards. Then they came out onto a clearing. Red saw a shallow water hole in the center of the clearing.

Manuel seemed to be groping in the air. His hand found something and he motioned for Red to feel. Red pawed in the darkness, then he felt it. A leather thong, tight and dry between two trees. A foot below it, he felt another. And then another. And then he realized that this small clearing was, in effect, a cleverly concealed corral with a rawhide fence. Manuel must have spent several days tying thongs of green rawhide between the close trees and when it dried it tightened up into a fence as strong as steel.

Manuel led the way around to the opening of the corral and pointed up to the limbs of a huge old mesquite tree. Up there just above the mouth of the corral was hanging a crude gate suspended by a single strap of rawhide.

Red could see how Manuel had been capturing so many wild cattle single-handedly. He perched up in the tree, naked and disguised to smell like a cow, and when the wily brush mavericks sneaked into this water hole to drink at night, he'd drop the gate on them! Red marveled at it. Manuel was the smartest brush *vaquero* that ever lived!

They crawled up into the mesquite. Talking was out of the question now. Red listened to the sounds in the brush, trying to pick out the noise of cattle. He heard the warbling of a mockingbird, the sudden barking of a coyote, the rustle of an armadillo. But an hour passed and not a longhorn showed a hair. Then another hour.

Red was getting cramped and he was tired of smelling himself. Suddenly Manuel reached over and squeezed his arm. Red looked in the direction the foreman was pointing. He strained his eyes, then saw it—an old bull with mossy horns that had a spread of at least six feet. He was coming cautiously down the trail, pausing now and then to sniff the air and to toss his horns. He got to the gate, just below Red and Manuel, then turned around and snorted softly.

Red held his breath, knowing that bulls usually didn't travel alone in the summertime. Sure enough, this one was bringing a dozen cows and a few calves with him. They broke into view down the trail where he had put in his appearance.

The old bull turned and moved into the water hole. Red saw him kneel, heard him drink, then pause to belch. The cows passed under the gate one by one. Now! Manuel yanked on a slip knot. The crude gate crashed down into its slot below.

In the corral all hell broke loose. The bull let out a thunderous bellow of fright and rage. He pawed the ground and charged the gate. When his horns crashed into it, the earth shook and Red almost fell out of the tree.

The cattle were milling around, bellowing. They butted the strands of rawhide, invisible in the dark. One tried to climb a mesquite tree on the edge of the corral and got halfway up, but he couldn't get over the top rawhide.

Manuel laughed in the dark, his teeth flashing, and clapped Red on the shoulder.

"What I told you, Rojo!" he yelled triumphantly. "We catch the cows, sí?"

"¡Sí!" Red breathed, his eyes shining. "¡Que bravo, hombre!"

They watched until the cattle had simmered down; then they started out of the tree.

Red was the first one down. He'd just got to the ground when the horsemen came out of the dark. They came in a bunch, all at once, out of the lane. Before Red could run for cover they were all around him, their horses milling and stomping. Men's voices cut the night above him, cursing. Red was stunned with surprise and then fright. These weren't Lazy R riders!

"Got th' thievin' varmint!" a man cried hoarsely.

Another man leaned from his saddle and a rough, gloved hand clamped on Red's arm.

"Why, hell, it's a kid. A nekkid kid. He ain't got a stitch on!"

"Lemme see."

Another man grabbed Red's arm. "It's Martinue's kid, that's who it is! Old Thirty-Thirty's kid!"

A surprised murmur went through the riders.

"That makes it all the better. Let's string him up right here. Show the old man we mean business!"

Red knew then who these riders were: Boxed X men, some of a new, tough bunch that Josiah Zepeda had put on to help him hold his range. They'd no doubt stumbled on Manuel's corral sometime today and stayed in the brush tonight, hoping to catch the Lazy R *vaqueros* who'd been using this corral. When they'd heard the trapped animals bellowing, they'd ridden here at a gallop.

"Hey, he probably had somebody with him."

"Yeah, look up in the tree and pull him down."

Some of the riders went around the mesquite tree. One of them hauled out his forty-five and blasted all six slugs up into the tree, bringing down a shower of limbs and beans. Red clamped his teeth and his fists, expecting to hear Manuel's body crashing down. But there was no Manuel in the tree!

The rider grabbed Red's arm again, hauled him

painfully half off the ground. "Who's with you, kid? You ain't come out here alone."

Red kept his jaws clamped. The man's other gloved hand crashed into his face. Stars splattered off in front of Red's eyes. "You answer me, you stinkin' little thief"

"You go to hell!" Red told him, his voice cracking.

"String him up!" the men yelled.

The one holding him grabbed a lariat and threw the loop over Red's head. Red kicked and struggled wildly, but the man kept a firm grip on his arm and yanked the noose tight.

Red gasped for breath. He wondered frantically where Manuel had gone. At the same time, he realized there was no way the Mexican foreman could save him, naked and unarmed as he was. They'd left their guns with the horses, several hundred yards back in the brush.

The free end of the rope swung over a limb.

"Now we'll show you what we do to cattle thieves, kid!"

"We got as much right to them cattle as you!" Red yelled wildly. "They ain't got no brand."

"They're on Boxed X range."

"They still ain't got no brand," Red yelled. "They're mavericks and you know I got as much right to them as you."

"Hell, pull the rope and shut him up. Ain't but one way to argue with that thievin' Lazy R bunch!"

Hooves rustled in the dry dust of the trail. The rope went taut. Red felt a painful, blinding jerk. He reached up and clawed at the rope.

All of a sudden there was a wild Comanche yell from the corral. It split the night. The riders whirled about. The man in the process of hanging Red dropped his rope and grabbed for his gun.

Things happened fast. The corral gate came crashing open in a cloud of choking dust. The old mossy horn and his cows, by now completely boogered, came charging at the opening. Their eyes were bugged out with fright, the whites showing, and they charged blindly, giant horns down.

Red moved with the instinctive speed of long years' training in the brush country. He leaped straight up, caught a low-hanging branch of the mesquite, pulled himself on it, and wriggled up higher.

From here he could watch the fun below. And it was something to see. The wild cattle came out of that corral like damned spirits who had just discovered the devil had left a gate out of hell open. They hit the bunched-up riders before they could get out of the way. Some of the Boxed X men got their horses into a dead run for safety, but others were caught broadside. Three of the men hit the ground and in the next instant were under drumming hooves and slashing longhorns.

Above the cursing and yelling and moaning, Red heard Manuel calling him. He saw the naked foreman out in the corral, waving frantically. He realized then that in the first moment of surprise when the Boxed X men had caught him, Manuel had crawled off the tree in the other direction and had hidden in the corral until an opportune moment, when he pulled the gate open. Red wasted no time getting out of the tree. He and Manuel streaked it through the brush, back to their horses and clothes. They rode naked for several miles before they stopped at a water hole to wash and put on their clothes.

Manuel had been cursing in Spanish in a steady stream ever since they left the corral. "You wait, Rojo," he said. "You wait an' see. There gonna be a fine fight purty soon. Those Boxed X *cabrones* are gonna start a bad war. Pretty damn soon. You wait an' see."

Red thought about Duncan Zepeda, the beating and the knife that had been taken away from him.

As far as he was concerned, the war had already started.

CHAPTER FIVE

There was no further trouble between the Boxed X and the Lazy R for a week. Thirty-Thirty's *vaqueros* combed the dense brush, chasing the wild mavericks out of their hiding places. Every morning the men left camp at sun-up, each rider equipped with a good *reata* and eight or ten *peales*, the short ropes that were used to hogtie the *ladinos* after they were roped. The Lazy R *vaqueros* could sneak their whirring *reatas* through the brush with incredible skill, somehow keeping the noose out of the thorny limbs that were everywhere.

When a wild critter was roped, the *vaquero* would tie him to some nearby brush with his *peale* and go deeper into the brush after his next quarry. Other riders would follow with lead oxen, and when they came upon a roped and tied maverick, they bound him to a necking ox and released the two. The lead ox worried the outlaw into obeying his lead; then he plowed full force into the brush, the two of them tearing holes right through the chaparral in a beeline back to the main camp's corral. The lead ox steer was eager to get back home to the treat of singed prickly pear or cottonseed that he knew would be waiting at the home corral. Occasionally the lead steer did not return with his charge. Then the men knew the outlaw had sulked and died somewhere in the brush and someone had to hunt up their trail and turn the lead ox free.

It was hot, thirsty, bitter work, wrenching those outlaws out of the stubborn brush one by one. But the job was completed by the end of that week. On the morning of the eighth day Thirty-Thirty and Red, both of them sore and stiff, rode around the big corral back near the home buildings of the Lazy R and looked over their roundup with pride.

The corral was filled with a milling, bawling hoard that filled the air with a rattling of horns and a thick cloud of yellow, choking dust. At one end of the corral there was a big mesquite fire blazing and turning a dozen Lazy R branding irons red hot.

Every few minutes the air was split by the outraged bellow of an outlaw longhorn as an iron burned into his hide. Gradually the air turned acrid with the smell of singed hide and hair.

It was along toward noon that a body of riders came stringing out of the brush toward the west and then bunched into a dusty knot crossing the open plain that surrounded the Lazy R buildings.

Red caught sight of them first. He called to Thirty-Thirty, who stood in his stirrups and squinted through the dust, then bawled an order to his Mexican ranch hands. In the corral the men dropped branding irons and grabbed rifles. They bellied along the powdery dust of the west corral wall, covering the body of riders.

Red figured they were Boxed X riders long before he could make out the blocky figure of Josiah Zepeda leading them. When they got closer, he also recognized Zepeda's son, Duncan. Red's teeth gritted and his fists bunched around his reins.

Zepeda rode up to within a few feet of Thirty-Thirty, his men in a body behind him, and stopped. "You can tell your hands in the corral to ease up on their trigger fingers, Thirty-Thirty," he said. "I'm not here for trouble. Not now, anyways."

Thirty-Thirty's eyes were frosty. His long tobacco-stained mustache drooped ominously. He sent a stream of brown juice across his saddle horn, splattering the front hooves of Zepeda's horse. "Maybe you didn't come fer trouble, but you got it, Zepeda," he said. "Some of yore cutthroats tried to string my boy up in the bresh last week."

The heavy-set owner of the Boxed X shrugged. "He was on my range, he'pin' himself to my cows. My boys have orders to stop that kinda thing."

"Yore range!" Thirty-Thirty snorted. "You got the deed with you to prove that, Zepeda? Hell, that there bresh ain't nobody's but th' rattlesnakes' and horned frogs'."

Zepeda put both hands on his saddle horn and rested the weight of his stocky body on them. "Thirty-Thirty, I was in this country with a ranch when you were still a saddle bum. I was running a herd in this brush ten years before you ever bought these buildings and the few acres around them. Maybe some of that land is open range, but the animals on it are mine. They're all descendants of my original herd. They belong to me!"

Thirty-Thirty howled, "Descendants of yore herd! Descendants of every Spanish and Meskin ranch west of San-tone, you mean. Hell, them mavericks could lay claim to bein' kin to any ranch you want tuh name."

Red was listening to the argument with only half an ear. With narrowed eyes, his gaze was riveted on Duncan. The son of Josiah Zepeda had taken a pocket knife out of his pocket. The sun flashed on it as he opened the fine steel blade. He tested the edge with his thumb, then slowly stropped it on the swell of his saddle. He looked at Red with an insolent smile and Red's blood boiled up in his head and pounded at his temples.

Zepeda was saying to Thirty-Thirty, "I didn't come to argue with you. I come to tell you for the last time, Thirty-Thirty. This range ain't big enough for us both. You're gettin' too ambitious. I don't like violence, but I'm goin' to protect my interests. I'm settin' a boundary between our range. The Mexican water hole. There's plenty of range on the east side for you. If you go west of that after my cattle again, I'm goin' into Laredo and hire the toughest gunslingers I can find and run you clear back to Wyoming!"

With that threat, Zepeda pulled his horse around and rode out of the yard. Thirty-Thirty sat in his saddle, resting on the horn. He gazed after the departing Boxed X riders. A stream of brown tobacco juice squirted from under his mustache. "Now I'm plumb scared to death," he said.

The branding was finished by the end of that week. At the start of the following week the herd boiled out of the corral, proceeded by lead steers and flanked and backed by the *vaqueros*. It stretched out like a fat snake, writhing through the dust, keeping to the open plains and less dense chaparral, west to the Rio Grande. They crossed a ford, swimming the horses and coaxing the cattle through the muddy water and up on Mexican soil. And then they turned the herd south through the white caliche dust and the waist-high chaparral, south to the Mexican coast and the Civil War contraband port of Bagdad.

That drive netted Thirty-Thirty the gold he needed to start his dreamed-of expansion in earnest. When he returned to the Lazy R, he enlarged the ranch house and built more sprawling corrals of mesquite poles lashed together with wet rawhide. He dug wells and hired more riders. And then he was ready to drive deeper into Boxed X territory.

Red was sixteen now and beginning to fill out. He rode beside Thirty-Thirty and the *vaqueros* into the brush after more cattle. And when they reached the Mexican water hole, Thirty-Thirty recalled the threat Zepeda had made a year ago, not to go west of this spot.

Thirty-Thirty had Red print a sign with a lead bullet on a piece of shingle tacked to a tree beside the water hole. The sign read:

ALL THE RANGE WEST OF THE RIO GRANDE
NOW BELONGS TO THE LAZY R.

Thirty-Thirty sat on his horse, admiring Red's neat lettering. "Yessir," he said, "there just ain't nothin' like a real school education." He punctuated the sign with a squirt of tobacco and pointed his horse west toward the Rio Grande. "C'mon, let's git us some more cows," he called to his men.

One night toward the end of that week, Red was just sitting down at the bunkhouse table for supper with the others when his keen ears picked up the drumming of hooves. Something rippled up his spine. He yelled a warning and grabbed up his plate and threw it at the lamp. A second after the room was plunged into darkness, there were orange flashes outside in the yard and the shaking thunder of gunfire. Glass tinkled. Wood splintered.

Red hit the floor and wriggled over to a chair where he'd left the gun belt he always wore into the brush. He reached up cautiously and pulled out the heavy Colt forty-five that Thirty-Thirty had been teaching him to use since he teethed on an empty brass cartridge.

He crawled over to a window with the gun.

He knew that the war with the Boxed X had really started.

CHAPTER SIX

Doctor Bruce Harrell left the saloon at dusk and started home through the muddy streets of the little Nevada mining camp. He had been drinking steadily ever since his patient died this afternoon at one-thirty.

He walked unsteadily, sometimes stumbling up to his knees into the muddy bog holes that rutted his path. The sixteen years since he had left New Orleans with Adrienne and their daughter Celeste had put a deep mark on his face. He was thin and his hair was grey. There was a twitching in his hands. His eyes were defeated.

They had seen sixteen years of drifting. He seemed unable to put down roots anywhere. There was never a lack of patients. Doctors of every kind were scarce in the frontier towns to which they drifted. But he couldn't build a permanent practice in any place they'd gone.

For sixteen years Adrienne had picked and nagged at the weakness in him, trying to make him charge his patients enough and collect his bills, trying to get him off whisky.

But he could never quite overcome the feeling of

inadequacy inside himself. He could convince his patients with the counterfeit diploma on his wall, but he couldn't convince himself. Whenever a patient died, which was often, owing to the lack of medicines in the frontier towns and the crude circumstances under which a doctor had to perform surgical operations, he remembered that he was really only a fraud, not a doctor at all. He'd barely completed half his medical training. Perhaps if he'd known more, he might have done better. He couldn't shake the feeling of inadequacy.

The inherent weakness in him had been made worse by the kind of life his indiscretion with Adrienne had driven him to. If he could have completed his medical training in New Orleans and returned to the safe, pampered plantation, to set up a practice among the genteel who knew and respected his family, he might have bumbled through life with a measure of security and success. But here, in these raw, new lands a man had only himself to fall back on, and that made Bruce Harrell a failure in his own eyes even before he was a failure in the eyes of others.

So he drank heavily to forget, and now forgetting and his beautiful daughter Celeste were the only things he lived for.

He arrived at half-past seven at the two-story frame house where Adrienne operated a boarding home. He carefully avoided the front door, stumbled around to the backyard, and let himself in through the back door.

Adrienne heard him bumping up the stairs and she

came up to their room as he was undressing.

"So," she snapped as she came into the room, "you went to the saloon again."

He took off his coat and put it over the arm of a chair. "Yes, my dear," he said, "I stopped by the saloon. But it's none of your damned business."

She put her hands on her hips. Her voice turned shrill. "You know what happened in the last town and the town before that and a hundred towns before that. People will put up with anything from a doctor but drunkenness. You don't have to know anything, not even how to make people well, but they'll believe in you because they want to. But you have to keep a professional air. People have no respect or confidence in a doctor that gets so drunk the sheriff puts him in jail."

He interrupted her tirade. "You know the Wilkins child? The one they brought in with the boil last week? I lanced it. Today they called me out to the house. Blood poisoning had set in where the boil was lanced. The child was all green and swollen. He died while I was standing there looking at it, wondering what to do—"

She came up to him and slapped him, first on one cheek, then the other. "Stop it!" she said through her teeth. "Stop doing that to yourself. So a child dies. Perhaps it would have died anyway. You did the best you could. Can you help it if they didn't keep the place clean? You're too soft to be a doctor. Too soft—too weak—"

"Leave me alone," he said wearily. He went to a bureau and took a bottle of whisky out of a drawer.

There was a sound in the hall. He suddenly shoved the bottle under some clothes and turned.

Celeste came into the room. She was almost grown now, almost a woman. He always looked with wonder at this beautiful child that carried his blood.

She came quickly into the room and kissed him, then wrinkled her nose, pressed her lips together and looked at him reprovingly. "Hello, Papa. You've been a bad boy again, haven't you? I could hear Mama fussing at you. You ought to be spanked." She turned to her mother. "Please help me, Mama. I can't get this dratted corset laced alone."

"A corset at your age," Harrell muttered.

"She's not too young to learn to look like a lady," Adrienne told him. "She's not too young to get married even, to the right man."

"Married! Now you listen—"

"Oh, be quiet. Come, Celeste. We'll go to your room."

He watched the two women leaving. He looked at Celeste, at the soft young curves of her body scarcely hidden in her lacy undergarments. She had the jet black hair and milky complexion of her mother, but a beauty in her face that her mother never had. She was perfection all over—her smooth, sun-browned arms, her dimpled shoulders, her firm bosom, her tiny waist and her long, shapely legs. A cold shock went through him. Adrienne was quite right. She was old enough now to marry and bear children. It was a frightening thought. She was all he loved and revered in life, and if he lost her—

The thoughts Adrienne put in the girl's head frightened him. Always she talked about marrying a rich man—warped thoughts for a child. He wished he could talk to her. But she was Adrienne's child. He couldn't talk to her. She wouldn't listen to anyone but Adrienne.

Later that evening, he found out why she had been dressing and primping so carefully. He heard her singing down in the parlor. By then he was quite drunk, but he got up and started downstairs so that he could hear her better. She had a voice like a lark.

When he reached the foot of the stairs, he could see past the tasseled drapes into the parlor. By the lamplight he saw her standing there, poised and lovely in the pink dress with the hoops that Adrienne had made for her. She was singing with her head tipped back slightly and the soft lamplight fell on her sweet young throat.

Then he became aware of someone else in the parlor with her, a man seated on the horsehair sofa, listening as his half-closed eyes went over her lissome body. The man was Leslie Kalinec, the wealthy man from New Orleans who had rented the biggest downstairs room a week ago.

Harrell swayed as he stared drunkenly at the scene; then he clenched his fists and started to the doorway. But Adrienne suddenly darted out of the parlor. She grabbed his arm, pushed him back to the stairway. He protested drunkenly, but she forced him back up the stairs with wild, angry strength.

Finally they were in the bedroom again. A strand of her hair had fallen across her face. She was perspiring and breathing hard. "You fool! You miserable fool! Coming downstairs like that. You pig!" She spat the words at him.

He said thickly, "I want to know what my daughter's doing down there singing for that man? What is my daughter—"

"She's doing something that might take her out of this miserable life," Adrienne hissed at him. "She's singing for a man who appreciates her beauty and her talent. Mr. Kalinec is wealthy. He owns plantations near New Orleans. He could give her everything. And you try to come barging in, you drunken, disgusting pig!"

He drew himself erect with sodden dignity. "Now you listen to me. She's my daughter, too. Leslie Kalinec is almost forty years old. Did you see how he was looking at her? She's still a child, an innocent child. I won't stand for an old man to look at my little girl like that. She's my daughter, too, you hear?"

"Your daughter! What have you ever given her, you weak, miserable failure? What have you given her but poverty and cheap, cold rooms and moving, always moving? Maybe you might give her some of your empty whisky bottles. That's something you could give your precious daughter. Oh, you fine, fine father, you!" She went out to the hall and slammed the door behind her.

He stared at the door for a long time, only hearing

the voice of his daughter still in song. She used to sing for him when she was a little girl. And now she was singing on the public auction block, parading before men like a woman offered to the highest bidder.

Harrell sat down, covered his face with his hands and wept. After a while he took a small derringer out of his bureau. He sat again, the gun in his hands. Lately, he'd held this little gun often—sometimes for an hour at a time. He had begun to think of it as a kind of medicine, a pill that would eliminate all his pain. All he would have to do was press the trigger and, magically, there would be no more pain.

He raised the gun and felt the cold round mouth of the steel barrel, like a woman's cool lips, touching his temple. Then he sighed and brought the gun down. He put it back in the bureau and poured a drink from a fresh bottle of whisky.

CHAPTER SEVEN

The Boxed X riders came into the Lazy R ranch yard like a bunch of howling Comanches that night. They had slipped up on the ranch quietly enough, but once sure of the element of surprise, they cut loose with everything they had.

Red crouched under a window of the bunk-house and cautiously peeped over the sill. Outside he could see the dark, phantom shapes of the Boxed X riders milling about in the ranch-yard as their guns blazed at the buildings.

Though Red was growing up in one of the toughest areas in the western frontier, he was still a boy and this was the first time someone had shot at him. He felt a cold lump in the pit of his stomach and his tongue stuck to the roof of his mouth.

"¡Cabrones!" Manuel Vera, foreman of the Lazy R *vaqueros*, shouted from the darkness of another window.

Red swallowed hard. He eased his forty-five over the sill and tried to steady it enough to get a bead on the shadowy riders. But the windows of the bunk-house were prime targets for the attackers. Splinters of wood flew from the sill near his hand. Ricocheting lead howled and thudded about him. He jerked back to the protection of the wall.

The Lazy R men, pinned down in the bunk-house, were firing sporadically from other windows, but it was a dark night and they had little to aim at but shadows. And the Boxed X men kept the windows under cross-fire.

Then there was light outside. A sudden burst of red and orange flame shot high into the night and sent grotesque shadows dancing the length of the ranch yard.

The men in the bunkhouse swore with frustrated rage as they hunkered under the windows and watched helplessly while the invading riders poured gallons of kerosene over corrals, feed sheds and barns; then ignited them with flaming torches.

They set fire to everything except the bunk-house and the main ranch house, which were built of adobe. Whooping and hollering like drunken Indians, they roped and dragged down fence posts and drove off the livestock.

When the attack started, Thirty-Thirty had been over in the main ranch house. Now, above all the noise, Red heard a bellow like that of a mad longhorn steer. He peered over the edge of the sill and his horrified eyes watched Thirty-Thirty fling open the front door of the ranch house and run out into the yard. He stood there spraddle-legged, his mustache bristling. He bellowed curses at the Boxed X men in two languages, punctuating every invective with a blast from a smoking forty-five clutched in each knotty fist.

Red choked on a frightened yelp. "Pa—!" Then he forgot about how scared he was. In a blind frenzy of concern over Thirty-Thirty's hide, he grabbed the bunkhouse door and ran outside. Manuel yelled at him and tried to catch him, but by then he was already in the yard, running toward Thirty-Thirty.

Lead was buzzing around him like angry hornets. It chewed the ground under his feet and howled around his ears and halfway across the yard it sent him skidding on his belly in a dive for the safety of a water trough.

Cautiously he sat up and peered over the splintered rim of the trough. With mingled surprise and relief he saw Thirty-Thirty still on his feet, sending a murderous hail of bullets at the men who had come to wreck his home.

When they set fire to the buildings and corrals of the Lazy R, Zepeda's hired gunmen had accomplished their main objective. But they also lost the protection of darkness. Now some of the riders were clearly outlined in the bright glare of snapping flames.

One of them rode past the trough. He was a stocky man astride a big dun-colored horse. There was so much light from the fire that Red could see a fluttering tab on the string of a sack of tobacco in his shirt pocket. Red became conscious of the heavy pistol still clutched in his sweating right hand. He slowly raised it above the trough and peered wide-eyed down the sights. He could see the man's dirty bandana handkerchief, his dark, sweat-streaked face. He was swinging a gun and yelling as he rode by the trough. Red followed him with his sights. Then his hand squeezed and the gun bucked with a deafening roar and flash of orange. The smoke stung Red's eyes. He saw the man jerk upright, then sprawl out of his saddle, landing on the ground with a bounce less than a dozen yards away.

Red stared wide-eyed over the rim of the watering trough at the man he had just shot. The big gun slipped out of his numb fingers and fell to the ground. His stomach flipped over.

Across the yard Thirty-Thirty was picking off Boxed X riders with deadly accuracy. He appeared to be in a hopelessly vulnerable spot as bullets ripped at his clothes and splashed dust against his boots. Blood trickled down his neck from a nicked ear lobe. Actually, he was in a better position than the invading riders, who were astride horses that were boogered by the gunfire and blazing kerosene. While they were slinging quantities of lead around, it wasn't with much accuracy and one after another of them was tumbling out of his saddle and none of them had yet got a straight bead on the angry old rancher. And now Manuel and his men in the bunkhouse were firing at targets they could see.

It added up to more than Zepeda's riders had stomach for and they spurred their horses out of the yard and disappeared into the brush with fading whoops.

They had lost some men, but they had left behind

a gutted ranch. Every wood building and corral was burned to the ground. The saddle horses and other livestock had been driven out into the brush.

In the silence that followed the last shot the Lazy R *vaqueros* slowly emerged from the bunk-house. Red stood up and moved around the watering trough. He approached the man he had killed, staring with wide, horror-filled eyes at the still form on the ground.

Then he suddenly became aware of Thirty-Thirty beside him. The old man shoved his guns into his belt. Gently, he laid his hand on Red's shoulder. "Lolita's been bad hurt, son. Better come in the house with me."

Red forgot all about the dead man on the ground. He stood frozen with panic. Now he knew why Thirty-Thirty had come charging out of the house in such a blind rage in the heat of the fracas.

Blindly, he followed Thirty-Thirty into the house. Lolita Flóres had been the only mother he'd ever known. Since the day she helped bring him into the world in the Red Lantern saloon, she had nursed him, cared for him, given him all the mother love of her generous, kind heart.

She was on a couch in the big room. She was wearing an embroidered blouse that Red had brought her the last time Thirty-Thirty took him to Mexico. Now it was stained dark with blood. Another Mexican woman, the wife of one of the *vaqueros*, was standing near her, weeping.

Red fell on his knees beside her. "*Mamacita—*" he choked. "Little mother."

She fingered a rosary with a trembling hand. Her eyes searched through the gathering darkness for Red's face. "Rojo, *mia*," she sighed. Her lips moved as she tried to say something else to him in Spanish.

The tears spilled down Red's cheeks. A wild hurting filled his throat. He looked at Thirty-Thirty desperately.

In the shadowy light from a single kerosene lamp the old brush popper's face was rawhide gashed with deep lines. "It was a stray bullet from one of their guns," he said gently. "There ain't nothin' we can do now, son. Even if we had the hosses, there wouldn't be time to ride to Cherokee Flats for th' doctor."

Thirty-Thirty had seen death often enough to know that it was in the room now, casting its shadow over Lolita Flóres' face. He moved to the fireplace and rested one fiercely knotted fist on the mantel, hiding the grief in his eyes from the others in the room.

Red closed his eyes, trying to squeeze back the tears. He knelt beside the couch, clutching Lolita's hand.

The room was quiet, except for the dying woman's breathing. With her last strength she held onto Red's hand. She had held him in her arms when he was a baby, had comforted him against her ample bosom, had fed him and cared for him when he was sick. She had filled his young ears with the colorful brush country legends and superstitions of her people. She had taught him Spanish before he knew English. Now she held onto his hand to the last moment.

Manuel Vera entered the room quietly. He crossed

himself and stood near the door, the brim of his brush hat crushed in his hands as he waited respectfully for the *patrón* to notice him. Thirty-Thirty looked up from the mantel and saw him. He nodded to his foreman and they stepped outside. The leathery-faced old rancher looked across his burned ranch, across the brush to the west and the direction of the Boxed X. "Send the men out into the brush," he ordered. "Round up the hosses, as many as you can get. We'll be riding at dawn."

"*Sí, Patrón,*" the foreman said. "*Con mucho gusto.*" He put on his hat and crossed the yard quickly. "*¡Andele, muchachos! ¡Pronto! ¡Vámanos!*"

The pink dawn was touching the uppermost dew-encrusted branches of the monte when Thirty-Thirty and his *vaqueros* rode to the west. They rode into the brush, stirring sleeping quail and frightening jack rabbits that scurried from before the horses' hooves. The air was still damp with the chill of night. A misty fog clung to the thickets and hollows and the horses waded through it, stirring it like swirling cotton.

Thirty-Thirty rode stiff and silent beside his foreman, Manuel. There was a quietness in the band of men. When a spur jingled, it was muffled, and the creak of saddle leather was a whisper. They rode into the *mogotes* of huisache and mesquite, and the branches rustled against scarred leather *chaparajos* and closed again behind the riders. One of the Mexican riders began softly singing a border song that told a story of death and vengeance and the evil spirits that followed where men rode.

Red was in his saddle with the *vaqueros* a short distance behind Thirty-Thirty, his eyes red, his throat still raw from crying. The *vaqueros* were careful not to look at him lest they offend the dignity of this man who had wept at the death of a loved one. True, he was a boy of sixteen, but he was also the *patrón*'s son, and last night he had run out of the bunkhouse and shot a *cabrón* of the Boxed X, a thing of much bravery. In the future they would tell the story as they sat around their campfires, and Manuel would act it all out, adding much to the glory of the *patrón*'s son.

They rode west until the sun had burned away the last of the mist and darkness in the monte and was hot on the back of their necks. They followed the trail the riders had made through the brush the night before after they had left the burning ranch yard. The trail led due west. It did not angle back to the Boxed X ranch headquarters, but pointed toward the Rio Grande and the Mexican border.

"*Ladinos*," Thirty-Thirty muttered. "Border *ladinos*. I didn't recognize a one of them stinkin' coyotes last night. They weren't none of Zepeda's reg'lar hands. He hired some *bandidos* to do his dirty work. Now they're heading back across the river. Prob'ly some of Cortina's cutthroats."

The brush country was infested with killers, rustlers, *bandidos*. The land between the Nueces River and the Rio Grande in Texas, the *brasada*, was open and lawless country. The Texas Revolution and the War of 1846 with the United States notwithstanding, the Mexican nation was still not entirely convinced that this was part of Texas at all. Bands of Mexican nationals led by the bandit Cortina made regular raids across the Rio Grande as far inland as Corpus Christi, killing settlers and stealing everything they could get their hands on. In retaliation, the Texans would go on regular Mexican killing sprees, shooting and hanging anyone of Latin blood that they ran across, often including perfectly innocent and loyal *Tejanos*—Texas-Mexicans.

A man like Zepeda would have had little trouble hiring a pack of Cortina's brush outlaws to burn the Lazy R ranch. All it took was gold or silver, and Zepeda had that.

The trail through the brush was clear enough. Apparently, the *ladinos* had thought they had plenty of time before the Lazy R *vaqueros* could round up their mounts and be ready to ride. Thirty-Thirty and his men even came across a campsite left by the *bandidos* where they had evidently stopped to water their horses, sleep for a few hours and make coffee.

Manuel swung down from his horse, felt the warm ashes of the campfire and estimated that the raiders were less than two hours ahead of them.

By late that afternoon that lead had been so cut down that the Lazy R riders sighted a straggler ahead of them in the brush. He saw them at the same time and fired through the brush at them, knocking the sombrero off the head of one of Thirty-Thirty's men. The cowboy swung easily down from his saddle without dismounting, scooped up the fallen hat, and then took out through the brush after the outlaw. Thirty-Thirty sent two other riders after him to help capture the straggler. In a little while the main body of Lazy R men arrived at a clearing and found that the three men had made their catch—and had already strung up their prisoner to the branch of a live oak with a *reata*.

"Chihuahua, he sure deed kick fine," the owner of the rope told Thirty-Thirty admiringly.

They rode fast now after the main body of raiders, hitting the brush at a head-on run, dodging the stabbing limbs and thorns, ducking, riding their horses in the expert manner of men who had fought the brush all their lives. When they sighted their quarry up ahead, a chorus of wild yells broke from the throats of Thirty-Thirty's *vaqueros*. There was some scattered gunfire, but mostly the fight broke into individual pursuits into the brush as the *ladinos* broke and scattered and were run down one by one. Most of the *vaqueros* ignored their guns, preferring to drag their opponents from the saddle and work them over with a knife.

When the fight was over and the survivors had been rounded up and questioned, it was determined that the original band that attacked the Lazy R last night had consisted of twenty-five men. Twelve had been killed in the raid and in this afternoon's brush fight. Five had got away and by now were no doubt swimming the Rio Grande as if the devil were in hot pursuit. Eight had been captured alive, but from the expressions on their faces it was evident that they didn't expect to remain in that condition for long.

Manuel had them brought to a clearing, where they were ringed with horsemen who had itchy trigger fingers. Thirty-Thirty leaned over his saddle horn and questioned the captured men in Spanish. They freely admitted that Zepeda had found them near Laredo and hired them to burn and destroy the headquarters of the Lazy R.

Some of them just stood there sullenly. Others, sweating profusely, got down on their knees and pleaded in broken English and eloquent Spanish for their lives. They called on their favorite saints and their dead mothers to witness their oath that they would never again ride across the Rio Grande if they would be spared.

Manuel was examining the lower limbs of a live oak in the clearing. "I theenk mebbe eso theese wan weel hold them O.K., *patrón*," he said, patting the tree with one hand while he held his *reata* in his other.

Thirty-Thirty squirted tobacco juice at a handy cactus leaf. "Nothin' would pleasure me more'n to watch 'em kick, Manuel. But I think mebbe we kin do ourselves more good by sendin' them back to their cousins with a leetle message."

Thirty-Thirty then ordered one of his men to build a hot fire of mesquite branches while the eight men were tied up to trees in the clearing. Then the rancher got stiffly out of his saddle and pulled out a Lazy R branding iron that he'd brought along and stuck it in the fire. The sweating captives stared at the iron with bulging eyes.

"Manuel, you talk better Meskin 'n me," Thirty-Thirty said. "You tell them so they'll be sure 'n understand. If we catch any *ladinos* in the bresh on Lazy R range, we brand 'em, and we don't stop to count whether they got four legs or two!"

Manuel grinned, fairly smacking his lips as he conveyed the information to the unhappy outlaws.

Red, sitting in his saddle beside Thirty-Thirty, watched the proceedings with wide eyes. The raw grief that had been an aching weight on his heart since last night had been half replaced by a burning need for revenge. An element of cruelty, an appreciation of the need for revenge, were deeply rooted in the character of the people who had raised and ridden with Red. Since he was a small boy he had listened to the camp-fire stories of these people, and their legends often told the accounts of revenge carried out with great justice and satisfaction.

Thirty-Thirty walked up to the first quaking outlaw, pulled out a Bowie knife and grabbed the man's left ear. The *bandido* howled for mercy. Then Thirty-Thirty proceeded to ear-notch him in the exact manner that the Lazy R cattle were earmarked. Blood squirted and the man yelled with great energy. But when Thirty-Thirty approached him with the cherry-red branding iron, the man's howls must have been audible to his relatives on the other side of the Rio Grande.

Thirty-Thirty yanked the man's shirt open and aimed the smoking iron at the exact center of his chest. The smell of burning flesh and hair arose from the branding. One of the *bandidos* fainted. Another began gagging and heaving.

Red watched the operation, trying to get some satisfaction as punishment was meted out to these men who had taken the life of his *mamacita*; the dull anger in him could be satisfied only by his own fists lashing out, striking, crushing something. What, he wasn't sure.

The branding of the outlaws was an impersonal thing, a simple matter of justice. He felt a bit sick, watching it, and he finally turned his horse and rode off a short way until it was over.

After Thirty-Thirty had branded the last of the bandits, they were released and they staggered and ran off into the brush. On foot they would be able to make it to the Rio Grande by the following morning.

When he was done with the branding iron, Thirty-Thirty cooled it in a small creek nearby and tied it behind his saddle. Manuel asked what his orders were. If he wished to ride against the Boxed X and burn their corrals, the *vaqueros* were willing.

Thirty-Thirty coiled his fingers around his saddle horn and gazed in the direction of the Boxed X. "Nothin' I'd like better," he told Manuel. "I'd like to put my brand on that Zepeda's stinkin' hide an' then string him up to a live oak. But he's too powerful for us, Manuel. He's got too many men on his place. He's still a lot bigger 'n us. I reckon the best we kin do now is ride back to the place, bury Lolita, rebuild the corrals, an' go back to ranchin'. Word of what we done will get back to Zepeda. It'll spread up and down th' border and through th' *brasada*. It won't be so easy for Zepeda to hire cutthroats to ride against the Lazy R the next time."

Red turned his horse back toward the Lazy R with the others, following them silently. But the deep anger still burned unsatisfied in him, and he rode with it as the sun sank and black night came to the monte with its sounds of owls and bull bats and the night varmints that rustled in the brush. At midnight the riders stopped and made camp. The men slept on the ground, using their saddles for pillows. Red looked up through the branches at the stars dotting the sky, and sleep wouldn't come because of the anger and the need to strike out against something.

He lay there while the dew soaked into his clothes and the stars moved in slow procession past the limbs above him. And gradually, the anger brought up the face of Duncan Zepeda. The grief of his *mamacita*'s death and the memory of Duncan Zepeda beating him to a pulp and taking away the prize knife became mingled together in his mind until they were one. And then his anger had a direction and goal. Duncan Zepeda was the son of the owner of the Boxed X and therefore a living part of the man who had paid the killers who shot Lolita. If his fists could hit Duncan Zepeda, he would be striking at the heart of the Boxed X—and avenging himself for the beating and humiliation he had suffered at the hands of Duncan Zepeda.

Very quietly he got up from the dew-wet ground. He found his horse in the darkness, saddled him, and rode off into the brush, setting his direction by the stars to lead him to the Boxed X. Since the beating near the schoolyard he had been afraid of Duncan Zepeda, but now anger had replaced fear.

It was almost dawn when he neared the Boxed X headquarters. He'd had no sleep for two nights and he'd spent all of yesterday in the saddle. His body was sore and gritty; his eyes burned as if sand were under the lids.

He tied his weary horse to a mesquite tree and approached the ranch buildings on foot. When he was near enough to see them through the brush, he made a burrow like a ground hog and lay hidden by the thorns and leaves while he kept a watch on the Boxed X ranch house.

The rising sun spread light across the ranch-yard, throwing the buildings into relief against the dark shadows behind them. Roosters began crowing. A hound crawled from under the back porch and stretched. The bunkhouse windows suddenly turned yellow from lamplight inside as the ranch hands crawled out of their cots. A man appeared in the doorway in his long underwear, gazing at the rising sun. He walked stiffly to the well back of the bunkhouse, drew a pail of water and splashed his hands and face and shivered.

Red lay perfectly still in the brush, watching the despised ranch come awake. It was a much bigger, much more powerful ranch than the Lazy R, and with twice as many hands. When the cook came out on the back porch and gave the breakfast call, a small army of *vaqueros* trooped across the yard from the bunkhouse.

Red thought of the mornings he had sat down with the Lazy R riders to eat Lolita's good *huevos rancheros*, and the pain stabbed in his heart again. Fresh realization swept through him that never again would he see her bustling around her kitchen, always with a smile of love for him in her eyes. He thought of the times he had been mischievous, had caused her pain and trouble, and how her large, beautiful brown eyes had only been patient in return, her hands gentle with love for him.

Hot tears rolled down his cheeks. His fingers dug into the earth. The ranch before his eyes had taken her away from him. A scalding wave of hatred welled up in him and fiercely his hands clenched fistfuls of the soft earth.

He lay in his burrow as still as a possum, never taking his eyes off the ranch. The sun grew hot through the network of thorny branches above him. Sweat trickled down his face and soaked into the ground under his belly. His tongue grew thick and heavy with thirst, but he didn't move. He had been trained by Thirty-Thirty and the brush *vaqueros* since childhood to know that a good hunter forgets all the minor discomforts of his body by focusing his entire awareness on his prey.

He saw the Boxed X men go to work after breakfast, some of them riding out into the brush, some breaking wild mustangs in the corrals, others doing blacksmith and carpenter work around the ranch yard.

He saw Duncan Zepeda with them. The boy had grown even bigger since he gave Red the beating and took his knife away. Seventeen now, he was big and hulking, with short-cropped blond hair and fuzz on his cheeks.

He rode out with a group of the riders and Red waited patiently. He came back with a freshly broken mustang in one of the corrals and Red continued to wait patiently. Then Duncan rode out into the brush on the new horse and at last Red moved. He crept out of the burrow like a shadow and moved back to his horse.

Red made a wide circle through the brush, moving carefully and silently. The horse he was riding had been trained to pick his way between and around and under the thorny limbs in the monte as quietly as sand running through fingers. Within fifteen minutes Red had circled the Boxed X ranch-yard and he could hear Duncan threshing into the thickets up ahead on his skittish, half-broken mustang.

Red nudged his horse and he moved faster. Soon he could see Duncan's checkered flannel shirt. He worked his horse through the brush quickly. Then they were in a small clearing. Duncan Zepeda suddenly twisted in his saddle, only then aware that he was being trailed.

Red saw his white, surprised face in a blur. Then he was beside him on a running horse and grabbing blindly, throwing his arms around the other boy, dragging them both out of their saddles as Duncan gave a surprised snort. They hit the ground with a thud that knocked them both momentarily senseless.

Red staggered to his feet half-dazed. Duncan Zepeda was trying to sit up. His shirt was torn and one side of his face was skinned. He blinked at Red vacantly.

Red shook his head to clear it. He looked down at Duncan Zepeda and all the wild anger of the past two days exploded inside him. He threw himself at the other boy, hitting, gouging, kicking in a blind frenzy.

The attack jerked Duncan back to his senses, but not before he'd got a bloody nose and a collection of bruises. The two boys rolled on the ground for a moment, snarling and gasping. Red grunted as Duncan's knee jolted into his stomach. Then he clamped his teeth into the soft flesh of Duncan's arm. He bit down until he tasted salty blood and heard the other boy yowl.

Duncan scrambled away from him. Then they were both on their feet, breathing hard and circling each other warily like a pair of wildcats. Their shirts were torn half off, their hair was matted with dirt, their faces were bloody.

The fall from the horses had jarred their pistols out of their gun belts. Duncan eyed one of the fallen guns now as he and Red faced each other.

Suddenly he made a dash and grabbed for the fallen gun. Red beat him to it, kicking it into the brush. But Duncan grabbed the kicking boot and yanked it waist high, throwing Red to the ground so hard the breath was knocked out of him.

Duncan took advantage of the fall and pounced his adversary. He threw Red over, grabbed his right arm and brought it up behind his shoulder blade, applying pressure to the cruel hold until Red gasped with pain. The Zepeda boy was half-insane with fury. He caught sight of a cactus bed a few feet away and pushed Red over to it, still pinning him down with the arm hold. Then he grabbed Red's hair at the back of his head and slowly pushed his face down toward the barbed prickly pear leaves.

Red was in a helpless position on his stomach. Duncan was about to twist his right arm out of the socket. Red was sobbing with pain. His wide eyes stared with horror at the clusters of thorns, inches from his face. Duncan pushed him farther down. The needle-sharp points reached up to Red's eyes, closer, closer, closer.

Panic choked him. His left hand clawed helplessly in the dust. Suddenly, acting on instinct, he grabbed a fistful of the dust with his free hand and hurled it over his left shoulder.

Zepeda cried out as the dust hit his eyes and for just a moment he relaxed his grip. Half-crazed with panic, Red moved with a burst of frenzied, superhuman strength. He managed to heave Duncan off his back and twist around and shove Duncan away with his knees.

The other boy was pawing at the stinging dust in his eyes. Still on his back, Red lashed out with his boot heels. The spur on his left boot caught Duncan Zepeda on the chin and laid his cheek open all the way up to his ear. Duncan fell back, dazed with pain. Red leaped to his feet. He swung his fists wildly. He felt his knuckles smash Duncan's face until the husky Zepeda boy had sprawled unconscious on the ground.

Then Red clawed through Duncan's pockets with trembling fingers.

At last it lay in his palm! The beautiful German-made knife that he'd won in the spelling match last year—the knife that Duncan had taken away from him!

He opened the big blade. Sunlight glinted on the polished, razor-sharp steel. He clutched the knife in his sweating palm. He looked down at the battered face of Duncan Zepeda and for a blinding second all the grief and blind anger welled up in him again. He held the point of the blade over Duncan's throat. He almost brought it down. But something very deep in him stopped his hand. Instead, he staggered to his feet, gave Duncan Zepeda a parting kick, and limped back to his horse.

As soon as Thirty-Thirty and his men awoke early that morning and found Red missing, they started out to trail him through the brush. But Red had been clever about covering his trail. Thirty-Thirty had taught him how to ride along the rocky bed of an arroyo where a horse left no hoof marks. They followed him until they came to an arroyo and then his trail vanished. Thirty-Thirty knew they might poke around in the brush for days before picking it up again.

The rancher made dark promises about what he'd do to the hotheaded young mustang when he laid his hands on him. He led the way back to the Lazy R ranch. They would sleep tonight and start out with fresh horses in the morning and search the brush until they found Red.

But that night as the men in the bunkhouse were shucking their trousers, getting ready for bed, they heard a horse picking his way into the ranch yard. Manuel grabbed his pistol and reached for the light. But the door opened. A battered figure stood there. His clothes were torn and stiff with dried blood. His face was pale.

He held out his hand. In the palm there was a beautiful pocket knife with a solid bone handle. "I really won that spellin' match last year," Red mumbled. Then he fainted dead away.

CHAPTER EIGHT

Josiah Zepeda continued to cuss Thirty-Thirty and to try and hold back the spreading Lazy R, if not drive it out of the *brasada* completely. But Thirty-Thirty and his son and their *vaqueros* clung tenaciously to the brush country and fought back.

During most of the Civil War Thirty-Thirty drove his cattle across the Rio Grande down to the port of Bagdad on the Gulf of Mexico. At the close of the war he looked around for new markets. He heard stories that other cattlemen were driving their herds north, all the way across the Texas and the Red River up to the railhead at Dodge City, where cattle buyers from the East were paying good prices for Texas beef.

"We're goin' t' round up th' biggest danged herd yet," Thirty-Thirty proclaimed, and his men spent the next two years digging enough cows out of the brush to satisfy his ambitions.

The longhorns that the brush country ranchers drove to market were as ornery as the thickets they lived in. Thirty-Thirty cussed them energetically, but deep down he felt a grudging admiration and affection for the cantankerous, wily critters. They refused to be dumb, driven cattle. They'd accept no master. They clung fiercely to their freedom and independence. When cornered, they pawed the dirt, shook their enormous horns, and glared defiance at their captor. They were pot-bellied, stringy, ungainly creatures, and sometimes when they had to choose between liberty or death, they just laid down and died.

They could be as wild as mountain lions. They would climb mesquite trees for the beans. They could run like an antelope, or suddenly squat in a *magote* and hide like a possum. They had to be hardy, fierce, and resourceful to exist in the arid, drought-ridden thickets of southwest Texas.

Some of them lived in the brush for thirty years and grew mossy old horns with an awesome spread. They could survive year-long droughts by sucking the moisture from prickly-pear leaves. Some of those prickly-pear eaters looked like porcupines until the thorns that had stuck in their heads decayed and festered out.

And the critters could be dangerous. Once, Red and three other *vaqueros* got a wild-eyed outlaw cornered on a creek bank. He turned on them, gored three of the horses to death and chased the riders up live oak trees. Red took to the creek and swam his horse to the other side for safety. The longhorn looked around, snorted once, and trotted off into the brush.

Thirty-Thirty and his riders employed all kinds of tricks to catch the brush cows. They used catch dogs, trained to know the scent of the longhorns, decoy herds of tame cattle to fool them, hidden corrals to trap them.

But most were caught by plain hard, dangerous work, a *vaquero* riding headlong through the brush until he could throw a rope on the outlaw. Sometimes a brush cowboy could knock some civilization into a rambunctious steer by "tailing" him. He'd chase the maverick until they came to a clearing, then lean down and grab his tail. Then he'd spur his horse into a sudden burst of speed so that he pulled the rear end of the longhorn around and crashed him to the ground with a jar that knocked the fight out of him. Often when the steer climbed shakily to his feet after an experience like that he was slightly cross-eyed and considerably more reasonable.

Other times the *vaqueros* tied forked limbs around the necks of the wilder cows or tied their heads down to one front foot, or sewed up their eyelids so that they'd blindly follow other cattle. To take the fight out of the worst of them they'd have to shoot them through the horns or chop the horns off with an ax.

Red grew to manhood during those two years of the big roundup in the brush as they got the large herd together for the cattle drive north to Dodge City. The brush made a man out of anyone who fought it, or he didn't survive. More than once it came close to getting the best of Red.

He was riding hard through the brush one day after a maverick heifer. When they came to a small clearing, he threw his rope over the cow's horns. He was astride a horse that was trained to squat and brace his hooves when a rope was thrown. The horse squatted, the rope tightened, and the cinch on Red's saddle broke. The saddle went over the horse's head and Red was still straddling it. He rode it for a hundred yards into the brush until it finally got too tangled in the limbs and thorns to go any farther and the rope stopped the heifer. She was old enough to have grown herself a pair of wicked horns. She turned and charged. Red climbed a tree in a hurry. Finally, the heifer got so tangled up in the rope and brush, she couldn't move. Red climbed down, sewed up her eyes with buckskin, and got her back to camp with a trained lead cow.

But the next morning he was so stiff that all his joints were locked. The *vaqueros* had to lift him to his feet and work his arms and legs before he could move.

At last the roundup and branding was done. They drove the motley herd northward, the scraggly, pot-bellied longhorns, still wild-eyed and savage from their outlaw days in the brush. They headed across the plains of the Choctaws, Kiowas, and Comanche nations. Red nursed the long-horns, cussed them, sang to them at night and, stripped down to his shivering hide, guided them across swollen rivers.

They went up through the hill country, the plains of north Texas and across the Red River. When at last they reached Dodge City, tired, gaunt, bearded and dirty, Thirty-Thirty slapped his son's shoulder and paid him the cowman's compliment of approval: "Son, you'll do to cross the river with!"

Thirty-Thirty was suffering from a tremendous two-year thirst. He got paid for his cattle in gold, more money than he had ever had his hands on before in his life. He paid off the *vaqueros*, gave Red his share, salted away a chunk in a bank for safekeeping, and took the rest of it into Dodge to raise hell with.

Red was twenty now and old enough to do some hell-raising of his own. For two years he'd been in the brush and on the trail, thinking about Dodge City as if it were the promised land. Cowboys riding back from cattle drives told exciting stories of the gambling, the beautiful women, the opera house. It was a big, whoopin', hollerin', ring-tailed carnival, going twenty-four hours a day. They had the dangdest machine you ever set eyes on in one of the big gambling halls, a cowboy had told Red. You cranked it up and put a coin in it and there was a drum and a fiddle and a tambourine in it that played music mechanically. Red sure wanted to see that dingus.

The Lazy R outfit was camped a mile outside Dodge. When Thirty-Thirty paid off the hands, Red took his money and rode into the trail city. He looked around with wide eyes; he'd never seen anything like it before. The streets were filled with traffic—wagons, horses, buggies—going in all directions. There were huge stockyards crammed with milling, bawling cattle. There was a depot where the trains came in blowing steam, all the way from the East.

And there were people. Red had never seen so many or such a variety. He saw dirty, bearded, wild-eyed cowboys fresh off the trail like himself. He saw Yankee soldiers in their blue uniforms, cattle buyers, city slickers, buffalo hunters, Indians, horse traders. And he saw good-looking women.

He slung his reins around the hitch rail in front of the biggest hotel in town and rented a high-priced room, throwing down gold coins on the desk to pay for it. He swaggered some because he was young and broad-shouldered, a big cattleman from Texas with gold in his pocket.

The hotel porter, a rheumatic old graybeard, wheezed up the stairs ahead of Red, packing some of his gear.

The hallway was covered with plush, wine-red carpet. Red had never seen anything so fine. His boot heels sank deeply into it and he walked gingerly so that his spurs wouldn't cut it.

Then, as he followed the porter down the hall, a door to one of the rooms opened and the most beautiful woman Red had ever beheld stepped out into the hallway. For a moment, before she moved away from the door and down the hall to the stairs, she faced him and her large, dark eyes met his fleetingly, driving a shock into him.

In age, she seemed close to him, around twenty. There was a blackness in her eyes as deep and secret as a moonless night in the monte. The size and swirling depth of her eyes held his gaze for the moment before he could clearly see her as a whole.

She was of medium height and her body was at the age when all the shadows and hollows and curves of her womanhood were at their most alluring. Her skin had the moist, dewy look of a girl on the threshold of womanhood. The women Red had known on the frontier of South Texas were burned brown and hard by the bitter, arid heat. But this girl's complexion was pale ivory, with a tinge of healthy pink that made it glow, and it was so delicate that it was translucent in places, revealing the faint tracing of blue veins under the surface.

Against the fair complexion, her eyes and hair appeared a startling jet black in the way that a creamy pearl on black velvet accentuates its dark background. Her face had a beautiful symmetry, with high cheekbones, shadowed cheeks, and the full red mouth of the sensuous woman.

She was dressed in a full skirt, made of a polka dot material that rustled softly when she walked. She stood with one hand on her doorknob, looking straight at Red for the time it took her bosom to slowly rise and fall once. Then she moved around him, her head down. She walked past him, so close he could have touched her. The delicate, bewitching scent of her perfume lingered in the air after she had gone.

With an effort Red shook off the spell her first glance had cast on him and followed the creaking old bellboy to his room.

"I don't reckon you'd know who that lady we passed in the hall was, would you?" he asked the porter with some embarrassment.

The old codger gave him a wicked, toothless grin. "I reckon I do, sonny."

"W-well," Red stammered, "w-what do you know

about her?"

The porter was busying himself opening windows and closet doors. He gave the pillows on the bed a slap, then turned to Red, one hand casually outstretched. "Any time I can be of service to you, mister, you jest lemme know," he said slyly.

Red got the hint. He deposited a gold coin in the outstretched palm. The porter turned it over happily. Then, as if sudden recollection struck him, he said, "Oh, you was askin' about Miss Celeste."

Red's cheeks were warm. "That her name? It sure is pretty."

"Oh, it sure is," the antique bellboy cackled. He poked Red in the ribs. "Makes a feller paw th' ground, don't it?"

"What else you know about her?" Red asked.

The septuagenarian's face went blank. He scratched his head with one hand while the other went out palm-up again. Red fed it with another gold piece and the old bandit's memory returned. "She's from New Orleans," he told Red. "Opera house hired her all the way up here to sing. That's whut she does, sing. Real purty, too. She'll be singin' there tonight. You kin buy tickets down in th' lobby if you're inter'stid."

The porter scratched the grey stubble on his chin, gazing at Red speculatively. He started to the door, then paused with his hand on the knob. "Course, her name ain't really 'miss' Celeste—"

"What is it, then?"

The old thief's mouth closed and his palm shot out.

Red's hand suddenly caught up the front of the man's jacket and he lifted the ancient bag of bones up, pinning him to the wall so that his feet danced several inches in the air.

"I was gonna tell you!" the man squealed. "Don't go gittin' all riled!"

Red put him down and the old man wiped a trembling hand across his forehead. "Her name's Mrs. Leslie Kalinec. That 'Celeste' were her maiden name. It's whut you call her stage name now."

Disappointment flooded through Red. "You mean she's married?"

"Ain't it always that way with the purty ones?" the porter said sadly. "Sure ruins it for us single fellers." Then he went on in a gossipy tone. "It beats me, though. Young an' good-lookin' as she is, married to this guy more'n twicet her age. Cain't see whut she'd want with a feller that old. Reckon he had money oncet, though, when she married him. I heard he was a rich Louisiana plantation owner; then th' war come along and now he ain't got nothin'. She's got to get out and earn the money with her singin'. He jest hangs around th' saloons, drinkin' all the time an' gamblin' an' talkin' about the old days 'fore th' war ruined him. I think he's a leetle touched in the head." Red sat down unhappily. All his good feeling had been spoiled.

The porter opened the door. "Want me to have th' desk clerk reserve a ticket for the opera house so's you kin hear her sing tonight?"

Red thought for a moment. Married or not, he had to

see her again. He nodded. "Get me a ticket."

The fate that twenty years ago had pushed Red Martinue into this world in a saloon in Cherokee Flats, and Celeste into the world in the French Quarter of New Orleans, had brought them together at last.

CHAPTER NINE

For the first twenty years of his life, Red's experience with women had been somewhat limited. Lolita Flóres had been the first female he'd known. Then he'd gone to school in Cherokee Flats and met the local girls his age, daughters of ranchers and businessmen of the town. At that age none of them had made much impression on him.

On the cattle drives into Mexico, Red had seen pretty, dark-eyed *señoritas*. And he had seen other women in San Antonio.

None of this, however, had prepared him for a girl like Celeste Kalinec.

He had the porter fill the copper bathtub in his room with steaming water and he scrubbed off the layers of trail dust and sweat. Then the hotel barber came up to his room and gave him a shave and a city haircut. He bought himself some good-looking new clothes, preparing for a big night. The whole time he was doing these things, he was not able to put Celeste Kalinec out of his mind.

He had himself a thick steak in the hotel dining room, then sauntered out into the streets to have a look at the wicked city of Dodge by night. Front Street, the main thoroughfare, was teeming with life. Even at night the stores were busy selling, trading, outfitting, and restocking. The boardwalks were jammed with people and the streets were filled with riders weaving in and out, freight outfits rolling into town, horses tied to hitch racks.

The air was filled with noise—the crack! of mule skinners' whips, the tinkle of pianos from the saloons, the high-pitched laughter of women, the low rumble of men's voices. There was a mingled smell of dust, horse leather, and cow manure on the night air.

Front Street ran parallel to the Santa Fe tracks. To the north, on a hill, was the residence part of town. And on an adjoining rise was Boot Hill, the town's cemetery. South of the tracks, between the Arkansas River and the railroad, was the tenderloin section, called "Hell's Half-Acre," a raucous collection of hurdy-gurdy houses and gambling halls, all doing a roaring business.

The whole town was geared to satisfy the trade of cowboys and the buffalo hunters. It was the last jumping-off place before the dangerous wilderness to the west, the end of the railroad, and the center of the buffalo-hide hunting trade.

Every day men streamed in, their pockets filled with money from buffalo hunting or trail herding, and Dodge City did its best to separate them from all that burdensome gold.

There was a constant stream of men heading from one saloon to the next, spurs jingling on their dusty boots, out to buck the tiger, dance with painted women and get drunk. Red joined them.

He found that Dodge City was an expensive town. He had to pay two-bits a shot for drinking whisky at the bar. He had a couple of drinks in The Road to Hell saloon, played faro, then had some more to drink. A young, redheaded dance hall girl latched onto his arm and got him to dance with her. She was good-looking and she pressed herself against him.

This was what Red had planned for the evening. After two years working the brush, then fighting the long, hard trail to Dodge with a herd of ornery, stubborn longhorns, a man was entitled to throw some money around and satisfy his hunger for feminine company. But somehow the redheaded girl held no appeal for him.

He left The Road to Hell and made the rounds of the other saloons and gambling halls on Front Street. In one he ran into Manuel Vera and his *vaqueros*, drinking tequila. In another he found Thirty-Thirty. The old brush popper was howling drunk. He had a young girl on each arm. Red didn't horn in on his fun, but he left the saloon grinning. He was beginning to feel a warm glow from all the drinking.

But the evening was falling flat for him. Every time he'd look at a girl in a saloon, a pair of wide dark eyes would flash across his mind. He'd thought that a few drinks would make him forget the dark-eyed beauty, Celeste, whom he had seen for only a few seconds. But the more he drank, the sharper her image became.

He finally admitted to himself that he wasn't going to get her out of his mind and he might as well go hear her sing—exactly what he'd been wanting to do all along.

The performance at the opera house was just beginning. Red had to take a seat near the back.

The orchestra began playing and Celeste stepped out on the stage. There was applause and whistling from the audience. A drunken cowboy in the balcony took out his forty-five and shot a hole through the ceiling. The management had him removed before the show went on.

Red was too spellbound to applaud. This afternoon, in the street dress, Celeste had been lovely. But now she was beautiful beyond anything in his wildest dreams.

Her black hair was swept up and gathered in a stylish coiffure. She was dressed in an evening gown the color of Burgundy wine. It was cut daringly low, revealing her lovely shoulders and the sweet, soft mounds of her bosom. When she sang, it was like the angels on judgment morning.

Red was sick with love. He was stunned, devastated, wrecked.

After the performance, he walked out of the opera house and stood on the sidewalk in a daze.

The crowd from the opera house moved about him and then he was standing there alone. One by one, the lights in the building went out. Red still didn't want to leave. He thought he might be lucky and catch a parting glimpse of Celeste as she left, so he wandered around to the alley in back of the opera house, where the performers' entrance was located.

It was dark here and Red decided he was too late. He started to walk away, but at that moment the door opened. For a second he saw her in the lamplight of the doorway. A man was with her. They left the building and stood in the shadows of the alley. They were talking in low, angry tones. Suddenly, there was a sound of a sharp slap. The man had hit her, knocking her against the building. She was huddled there, sobbing. He grabbed her arms and shook her.

Red was frozen for one second. Then, wildly, he ran toward them. He grabbed the other man's shoulder, swung him around. His fist crashed into the dark blur of a face. The blow knocked the man across the alley and he crashed into an empty barrel, splintering it, and then lay still among the wrecked hoops and staves.

Celeste was petrified with shock. She stared at the fallen man, her trembling fingers against her lips. Then she ran and bent over him. She turned to face Red, her bosom rising and falling swiftly. "You fool!" she gasped. "Who are you, anyway?" Without waiting for an answer she grabbed his arm. "We have to get away from here before he comes to and sees you."

Red let her pull him to the end of the alley. When they were on the main street she could see his face. Her eyes looked puzzled for a moment. Then she remembered. "You're that cowboy I saw in the hall this afternoon."

"Y-yes, ma'am," Red gulped.

"What on earth were you doing in that alley?"

"W-well, ma'am," Red stammered, "I heard you sing tonight. You see, I thought maybe—"

But she was too agitated to listen. She kept glancing back to the alley as if expecting the unconscious man to come after them any minute.

Impatiently, she took Red's arm again. "We don't have time to stand here talking. Please take me back to the hotel." Her dark eyes were filled with fright.

"Yes, ma'am," Red said. "Only, don't you think we ought to go to the sheriff first? That man that attacked you is liable to come after you again."

She shook her head and walked fast, tugging at his arm.

Red tried to hold back. "Really, I think th' sheriff—"

"Listen," she said through her teeth, "the man you knocked down back there was my husband!"

Now Red stopped walking completely. He stood in the middle of the sidewalk, staring at her. "You mean your own husband hit you like that?"

The red mark of the blow was still on her face. She said angrily, "It was a personal, family matter. I'm not going to stand here and explain it to you!" Then she sighed impatiently. "Look, cowboy, I do appreciate you coming to my rescue like that. It was gallant. But my husband can be very mean-tempered, especially when he's drinking. If he comes out of that alley and recognizes you, there'll be serious trouble. I can't stand any more trouble," she said raggedly. Then she turned on her heel and crossed the street.

Red ran after her. "I won't cause you any more trouble, Miss Celeste. But I would like to see you back to your room at the hotel."

She didn't speak to him again, but she let him walk beside her. When they reached the hotel, she thanked him briefly, but asked him not to come into the lobby with her, because they would be recognized. She seemed very frightened.

When she had disappeared into the hotel, Red slowly walked to the nearest saloon. He had a drink while he thought over the startling events of the last few minutes. Every time he thought of a man abusing a sweet, beautiful young wife like that, his fingers balled angrily.

He had another drink and got even madder. He thought about that beautiful girl alone in her hotel room, frightened and crying, waiting in terror for her husband to come home and hit her again. He had another drink.

By midnight he was too drunk to be wary. He walked unsteadily back to the hotel. He tiptoed along the soft carpet and then stood outside her door, listening.

He wasn't sure if he heard her crying in there. He suddenly tapped on her door. "Miss Celeste," he whispered. There was no answer. He tapped louder.

The door opened. Her face was a pale blur in the dim hall light. Her black hair tumbled in a loose mane down her back. She was wearing a thin robe, which she held together at the neck with her left hand.

"What do you want now?" she asked in a low, angry

whisper. "Are you just dead-set on getting all of us killed?"

He took off his hat respectfully. He swayed a bit, rocking back on his heels, and he reached out to the wall to steady himself. "I was real worried about you, ma'am," he replied in a whisper loud enough to be heard down at the desk. "I just couldn't get no rest tonight unless I made sure you were O.K."

She looked at him angrily. "You're drunk," she said. But then her eyes softened. "But you are sweet." She pulled him out of the hall, into her room, softly closing the door. Bright moonlight spilled through an open window, bathing her in a pale light.

She looked up at him, shaking her head. "Sweet, but dumb. What am I going to do with you, my brave cowboy?"

"Well, ma'am—"

She quickly put her fingers against his lips. "Everybody in the hotel will hear you. Now listen. You don't have to worry. My husband is still out somewhere, drinking. By the time he comes home, he'll be ready to quietly pass out. If you really want to help me, you'll just go to your room and not interfere any more tonight."

Red nodded meekly. But he didn't move. He just stared at her in the moonlight and tears came to his eyes. "I swear," he said softly, "I never seen anything so beautiful in my whole life. If you were my wife, I'd get down on my hands and knees and thank the good Lord for makin' you mine an' I'd treat you like a queen—because that's what you are, ma'am." He rocked back on his heels.

She gazed at him and her big eyes softened even more. "You Texas cowboys," she sighed, shaking her head. A smile tugged at her lips. "Big, rough, uncouth. And inside, the heart of a poet." She looked at him thoughtfully. "You just got off the trail today, didn't you, cowboy?"

"Yes, ma'am."

"Have you kissed a woman yet?"

"Why, no ma'am. I never—"

"Don't be shy," she reproached him gently. "You see, I understand men."

She continued to look at him speculatively, smiling. "Here, then," she whispered. She moved to him, slipping her arms around his neck. She stood on her toes so that her lips would reach his. For a second he felt her warm, sweet breath against his lips. Then her mouth touched his.

He blinked with surprise. Then he closed his eyes. Gingerly, as if she might break, he put his arms around her. He tasted her mouth, sweet and responsive for a moment. He could feel her warm body under the thin robe.

Then she rested her face against his broad chest. "You are trembling, *mon chéri*," she whispered. "Like a little boy." She stepped back from him. "That was wrong, because I am a married woman. But I wanted to thank you for risking yourself to help me and for being so sweet and kind. And how else can a woman thank a man?"

She pushed him to the door. "Now it will be our secret, but you must promise never to speak to me again, or act like you even know me. Promise, if you really like me and want to help me."

Red let her push him into the hall and then he walked blindly to his room. He fell on his bed without removing his boots. But he couldn't sleep. Her kiss burned on his lips like fire.

CHAPTER TEN

Red finally slept. Celeste came to him. She was a vision over his bed. The moonlight was soft on the curves and shadows of her and her gown was gossamer. Her hair fell loosely over her shoulders, spilling down to brush his cheek. And then he awoke and it was a dream—

He wandered aimlessly around the town all morning, staring at the sights but seeing the girl. He swore at himself because he had no business filling his mind with thoughts of a woman forbidden to him. She was another man's wife.

When he returned to the hotel early in the afternoon, the desk clerk told him that a deputy sheriff had been looking for him. "Somethin' about a feller named Thirty-Thirty Martinue that they got locked up in jail. He any relation to you?"

Red nodded and went down to the sheriff's office.

"We'd be glad to get him off our hands," the deputy sighed. "He's a-cussin' an' carryin' on so much that none of the other drunks in jail can git any rest. But somebody's got to stand good for the damages before we can turn him out. He gave us your name. Said you'd prob'ly be stayin' at one of the hotels in town."

"How much is the damage?" Red asked.

The deputy took a list out of a desk drawer. "Lemme see now. He broke a back-bar mirror in the Dead Meskin saloon with a whisky bottle. And there's the fire he started when he shot at the big glass chandelier in The Road to Hell. Then there's this dress he tore off the girl down at Sadie's place in Hell's Half-Acre. She claims it were brand new. Jest bought it yestiddy off a drummer from St. Louis—"

He ran down the list with a stubby pencil, probing his cheek with his tongue while he laboriously added up the price of the damaged items. "That there comes to two hundred and ten dollars altogether," he said.

Red paid him the total amount in gold coins. The deputy then picked up his keys and led the way to the jail.

Thirty-Thirty came blinking out into the sunlight, swearing at the Yankees that ran this town and proclaiming himself ready to shake its dust from his heels and head back to Texas, where a man could have some innocent fun without being thrown into jail.

But Red wasn't ready to leave Dodge. After some fruitless argument with his son, Thirty-Thirty gave up and rode out of town to the Lazy R camp to wait until Red took it in his head to start back to Texas.

That night Red went to the opera house again, drawn by the spell that the beautiful Celeste had cast over him. This time he sat in the front row and his hands grew sweaty and his heart pounded with anticipation as the curtain slowly went up and applause burst over the opera house. Tonight Celeste wore a gown of black velvet, a contrast against her bare shoulders and throat.

She bowed low, her gaze touched the front row, and she saw Red. For a moment their eyes met and held. He saw her flush, her hand move to her throat in an unconscious gesture. Then she looked away, giving the signal to the orchestra leader with a flick of her eyes.

Red sat through the performance in an ecstasy of longing. Afterward, he stood near the opera house in the shadows of the street until he saw her leave on the arm of her husband. Then he headed for the nearest saloon and got so drunk the bartender finally had a couple of men carry him out back to the livery stable and throw him in a pile of hay, where he slept it off.

The following day Red saw Celeste's husband, Leslie Kalinec, up close for the first time. It was in the hotel dining room at the noon mealtime. Red took a table near the door and then he spotted Celeste and her husband across the room.

He stared at Kalinec, trying to understand what had ever possessed such a young beautiful girl to pick this man for a husband. He was middle-aged. There was a trace of handsomeness lingering about his face, but there were soft pouches under his eyes and deep lines. His skin had an unhealthy pallor. He looked sullen, irritable, and his hand shook as he raised a water glass to his lips. He was dressed well, in the manner of a man who was used to fine things. His suit was of an expensive-looking dark material and there was a heavy gold watch chain across his vest. But Red wondered, with a stab of anger, if he'd bought the fancy duds with the money Celeste earned by singing.

Then his gaze moved across the table to Celeste and his throat tightened. Every time he saw her, she was more lovely. She was eating slowly, in a very proper manner, her eyes lowered as her husband talked to her in a low, sullen voice. Today she was dressed in a deep red velvet with a bit of white lace over her bosom, and a saucy hat of the same material. The color brought out the soft flush in her cheeks.

Celeste and her husband finished their meal and started to the door. As they did she faced Red and her eyes widened. Their gazes locked, held by some kind of deep current. Red's hands trembled as she moved past his table, so near her dress brushed his leg and her perfume reached out to him like an intimate whisper.

He saw them stand in the lobby for a moment, talking, and then Kalinec put on his hat and strode out of the hotel while Celeste walked up the stairs to her room.

Red left his table without ordering dinner. He walked up the stairs and stood in the hall outside her door. He wiped at the perspiration on his forehead. He drew a deep breath and knocked at the door. He heard the rustle of her dress. "Who is it?" she asked, her voice muffled by the door.

"It's me," he said, "you know, the Texas cowboy from across th' hall."

There was a moment's silence; then Red heard the

lock being turned. She looked up at him, her eyes wide, her face pale.

They stood there for a moment, neither speaking. Her fingers were pressed white on the door edge. She bit her lip, glanced past his shoulder, up and down the hall with frightened eyes. Then she stepped back and he came stiffly into the room, clumsy with the need for words.

He could see a tiny blue artery in her white throat beating swiftly. "You must leave right away," she whispered. "My husband will be back in a few minutes. He's been in a terrible mood ever since you hit him in the alley the other night. I made up a story about not knowing who you were. A stranger—a drunk, I told him, who got him mixed up with another person. But I—I don't think he completely believes me—"

Her voice trailed away. Her eyes looked bigger and darker than ever, staring up into his. Then they became flustered and suddenly lowered in consternation.

They stood in silence, a few inches apart, and Red could feel the warmth of his body taking possession of him. He could sense the same excitement in her. It gave him the courage to blurt out, "I want to see you someplace alone. Where—where we could talk for a while and it would be safe—" Then, with the words spoken and hanging in the air between them, he held his breath.

She stood before him, startled and frightened, breathing swiftly. She chewed her lower lip, darting glances from the corners of her eyes, in a nervous, frightened manner. Finally, in a low voice, she murmured, "The opera house will be closed tonight. Leslie will be somewhere drinking and playing cards. I'll be here alone most of the night. Maybe we—we could go for a ride somewhere—" Her head was bowed as she talked. A flush was on her cheeks.

Red felt a leap of happiness in his heart. "I'll get a buggy from the livery stable."

She nodded, her head still bowed. "I'll meet you behind the hotel. Eight o'clock—" Then she opened the door. "Please—leave now. Hurry." She turned her back to him.

Red rented the best rubber-tired buggy in the livery stable, and a handsome sorrel mare to pull it. At eight o'clock that night he was anxiously waiting in the deep shadows of the alley behind the hotel, dressed in the brand-new broadcloth suit and fawn-colored Stetson he'd bought that afternoon.

He heard the rustle of silk and saw a figure move out of the shadows. Then she was beside him. "Please hurry," she whispered. "Drive out of town where we won't be seen." She pulled a veil down from her hat to cover her face.

Red slapped the leather reins against the sorrel's rump and they rode out of town without speaking. There was only the sound of the horse's trotting hooves, the soft creak of leather and the rumble of buggy wheels.

The full moon spread silver over the plains of Kansas. The dirt road snaked ahead of them across the prairie. A mile from town they came to a small creek and Red pulled under the seclusion of a grove of cottonwood trees.

They sat in the buggy in silence. For Red the air was charged with the beauty of the girl. Her perfume made it sweet and the moonlight fell on her throat. He had never known a man could be so sure on a horse, so rough with cattle, so unafraid of a fight, and yet so paralyzed by a beautiful woman. All he could do was look at her and feel the longing and the hot wave that rose inside him. He had thought of nothing but being with her like this since he first laid eyes on her and now he couldn't find his tongue.

Her face was turned away from him. She was gazing at the moonlight that spilled through the leaves like silver coins. "I'm so ashamed," she whispered. "This is a terrible thing for a married woman to be doing. I must have lost my mind—"

Red didn't know how to answer her.

"I don't even know your name—"

"It's Red Martinue," he told her.

She looked at him with a curious expression. He saw the mood in her eyes change and become amused. "Red?"

He shifted self-consciously. "Does sound kinda odd with my dark hair, I guess." He blushed. "You see, I was born in a saloon—the Red Lantern. My pa named me after the saloon."

"Born in a saloon?" she giggled.

His ears felt hot. "Don't go hoorahin' me—"

Her hand moved to touch his. It was small and warm

and Red felt a shock at the touch.

He guessed she felt it too, because she quickly drew it back. "Let's—walk down to the creek."

Red tied the horse to a tree so that he could graze and they walked down to the creek bank. It was white sand, and the clear water trickled over a rocky bed. In the moonlight the wet rocks gleamed like silver and the water sparkled like diamonds. "Oh, look!" she exclaimed with the excitement of a small child. She knelt at the edge of the bank and touched the rippling water. Then they sat side by side on the sand.

"Not much water where I come from," Red told her. "Unless you go down to the Gulf of Mexico, of course."

"I was born near the biggest river in the whole world," Celeste informed him proudly. "The Mississippi."

"I learned in school there's a bigger one. Someplace in South America."

"I don't believe it," she pouted. Then she hugged her knees and rested her cheek on one knee, with her head cocked sideways so that she looked at him from a corner of her eyes. "Red-Named-After-a-Saloon," she teased him and giggled again.

Red blushed and jabbed a stick in the sand. "You know, sometimes it's kinda hard to think you're a married woman. Sometimes, like right now, you seem like a little girl."

The merriment left her eyes and they became sober. She turned her face, resting her chin on her knees, gazing sadly at the creek. "I know," she sighed. "I'm really not like this very often. I suppose I just felt happy for a change."

Red was silent for a moment, jabbing his stick in the sand, trying to get up the courage to say what was on his mind. Finally he did. "Why did you ever marry an old man like Leslie Kalinec?" he asked. "It's plain to see you don't love him! You're scared of him and unhappy."

"What makes you think I'm unhappy?" she asked in a muffled voice.

"You as good as admitted it," he insisted. "Besides, anybody can see—"

She was silent and then he saw tears trickling down her face. "It's a long, sad story, Red-Named-After-a-Saloon."

"I wish you'd tell me," he said.

She gazed moodily at the rippling creek. "Well," she sighed, "you won't think much of me after I tell you, but I guess that doesn't make any difference. We'll probably never see each other again after tonight." She was thoughtful, then began her story. "You see, Red, my mother was once a very beautiful and ambitious woman. But my father—well, I guess he wasn't much. He was a doctor of sorts, but not a very good doctor, and he drank too much. We traveled all over the West while I was a young girl, always going to a new town where he could start a practice, and then leaving when he failed. All the years I was growing in those crude, rough frontier towns, my mother told me about the beautiful city of New Orleans, where I'd been born. One day, she promised me, we'd have a lot of money and go back there and live in style in a fine plantation with slaves and horses and pretty clothes. But we never made it."

She fell silent for a few moments. Then she said, "Well, when I was sixteen, we had settled for a while in a town. We had this big house and mother took in boarders. One of them was Leslie Kalinec. He was from New Orleans and he was quite wealthy then. He owned a big plantation. He had taken a trip through the West for his health. He—well, my mother encouraged me to—to be pleasant to him. I sang for him in the evenings. I guess by then Mother knew we'd never get anywhere. My father was a failure. She meant well, I know. She just wanted good things for me. And Leslie was much nicer-looking then and—and much kinder—"

Red felt a hard knot in his chest and his fingers dug into the sand.

She went on doggedly. "I was too young to know much about marriage. When Mother told me that Leslie wanted to marry me, to take me back to New Orleans and give me all the wonderful things she'd always told me about, well, I thought it was the best thing that had ever happened to me. I was too young to know what love was really supposed to be. And I was happy—at first. Leslie was kind to me then. He really did have a beautiful plantation. It was like all the dreams coming true that my mother had put in my head. But the war was going on. Leslie couldn't sell his cotton on account of the blockade. His slaves began running away. The

Yankees took New Orleans. He lost everything he had. I think it did something to his mind. He's changed now. He drinks all the time. He's so mean. I'm—I'm just scared all the time. My parents are dead now. I have no one to turn to—"

Red swallowed hard and his fists were tight. He felt a kind of hopeless anger building up in him.

Celeste trailed her finger in the sand. "Well, we had to live somehow," she went on, completing the story. "I could sing. I was young and pretty. Leslie still had connections with people. He arranged for places that paid me to sing—opera houses, theaters, saloons. For the past six months we've been living like this, traveling from one town to another, living on what I earn, while Leslie gambles and drinks himself to death. And I guess I'm right back where I started." She smiled ruefully.

"I knew you were in trouble and sad," Red said, his jaws tight. "You ain't got any business stayin' married to a man you're scared of, supportin' him."

She sighed. "Well, I guess I made my own bed. Anyway, he's my husband, so I have no choice. He's crazy jealous and he'd never let me go. Every time another man even looks at me, he goes into one of his rages. That's the thing he's usually angry with me about, although I've never given him any real cause— at least not before tonight." She flushed guiltily. Then in a sudden, swift change of mood, she brushed the sand from her fingers. "That's enough sad stories for tonight! I want to forget my troubles and laugh for a little while. I never have any fun any more—"

Impetuously, she kicked off her slippers. Holding her full skirt above her ankles, she waded into the stream. "Oh, it's cold!" she gasped. Then she cried, "I haven't done this since I was a child. It's so much fun!"

Red sat on the bank, laughing, completely entranced.

She waded over the slippery pebbles and smooth flat rocks in the bed of the clear stream. Then she came to the bank and sat beside Red. Her feet were naked and wet. He dried them with his handkerchief and rubbed them until the warmth came back. His fingers trembled, touching her bare ankles and the hot wave of longing rose in him.

She had fallen silent and her huge eyes were regarding him solemnly. "You're so tender," she whispered. There was a tremor in her voice.

He looked up at her face, so beautiful in the moonlight. Her eyes met his steadily, excitement growing between them and warming their blood. He saw deep shadows swirling in their black depths, fright struggling with desire.

Then he suddenly took her in his arms and they kissed roughly. It was like an explosion between them. Her mouth was hungry against his. She trembled, her arms tight around him. A moan escaped her lips.

Then, she tore herself away from him, pushing her shaking fingers into her hair and sobbing.

"Celeste—"

She shook her head violently. She covered her ears with her trembling hands. "Don't say another word to me, Red," she pleaded brokenly. "I've already done enough tonight to be ashamed of. Please, take me to the hotel right away, if you care anything about me at all—"

They rode back to town, silent, the way they had come. But after a while, her hand slipped into his, and held it tightly.

"I have to see you again," Red said. "We have to—to do something. I'm not goin' to let you keep living with a crazy man. Maybe he'll hurt you bad some night—"

She shook her head. "It's hopeless. You'll only get us both killed. You don't know Leslie." Her hand squeezed his. Moonlight glistened on the tears in her eyes. "Go back to Texas, Red-Named-After-a-Saloon. Forget about me, please—"

They had reached Dodge and he had to give up the argument for now. He stopped the buggy behind the hotel and helped her to the ground.

They walked toward the back of the hotel, holding hands like young lovers who had just met. A figure moved away from the shadows and confronted them. Leslie Kalinec held a gun pointed at Red's heart.

CHAPTER ELEVEN

For a second they were frozen. Red heard Celeste's frightened gasp.

"Get up to the room," Kalinec ordered her.

Red moved a step toward him. "Listen—"

Then he saw the look of insanity in the man's face. Kalinec's eyes were yellow and blood-shot. His cheek twitched. "Cowboy, you're just one step from hell," he whispered, pulling back the trigger of his forty-five.

Red stopped, realizing that the man was out of his mind. Celeste's face had gone dead white. She whimpered with fear.

"I told you go get up to the room," Kalinec rasped at her. "Or do you want to see your boy friend's insides spattered all over your pretty dress?"

She darted a frightened, white-faced glance at Red, then ran to the hotel.

"Unbuckle your gun belt," Kalinec ordered. "Careful with your hands."

Helplessly, Red obeyed. His gun and holster fell in the dirt.

"Now kick it over here. That's right." Kalinec scooped up Red's gun, never taking his eye off him.

"I have friends around the hotel. They've heard you talking to my wife, in our room when I was out," he rasped. "Get on your horse, cowboy, and start back to Texas tonight, unless you're tired of living. Because if the sun rises on you in this town tomorrow morning, I'm going to kill you—"

He backed away into the shadows, keeping Red covered, then disappeared into the hotel.

Red stood there shaking with impotent anger. He knew he'd been a hair's breadth away from being gunned down, but even more than fear for himself was the terror he felt for Celeste.

But before he could do anything to help her, he had to get a gun. He ran out of the alley to Front Street. He found a hardware store that was open for late business and bought a Colt forty-five and a box of shells.

Red shoved the loaded gun into his belt under his coat. He strode into the lobby of the hotel. The desk clerk stared at him. He went up the carpeted stairway, covering three steps at a time with his long legs.

When he reached Kalinec's door, he could hear the man's angry cursing and Celeste's sobbing. At that same moment a man who had been standing at the end of the hall looking out of a window came over and stood before him.

The man, a buffalo hunter, was slightly over six feet tall and weighed close to three hundred pounds, every ounce of it hard beef. The greasy tan buckskin and moccasins he wore smelled like a mixture of rancid lard, tobacco, and dead buffalo.

Short fiery red hair stood up all over his head in unkempt tufts. One cheek was bulging with a load of tobacco. Freckles dotted his face, and his pale blue eyes were almost buried in folds of puffy fat. He studied Red's face blandly.

"Evenin', friend." He smiled, smacking his lips over the tobacco. "Guess you got your rooms mixed up, hum?"

Red frowned. "I don't reckon that's any business of yours, mister."

The buffalo hunter smiled happily, making sucking noises over his wad. "Your business, my business. Man never knows who's business is whose anymore, does he?" He was carrying a heavy Sharps buffalo-hunting rifle slung in the crook of his arm and he swung it around casually, between them. "Maybe you just better go on off to bed in your own room and we won't have to worry no more 'bout business, hum?" He grinned.

Then Red realized what this man was doing here. Kalinec might be crazy, but he was nobody's fool. He'd expected Red to come charging after him like a wild young bull on the prod and had picked up this rough character to stand guard at his door. Dodge was crawling with cutthroats who could be hired at the drop of a hat for a few gold coins.

Red stepped back and his hand went to the Colt stuck in his belt.

The buffalo hunter chuckled. "Say, you Texas fellers are real cards. Ain't them Texas fellers cards, now, Pete?"

"Yeah, Billy."

From the corner of his eye Red saw a half-breed Indian move catlike out of the darkness of a doorway aiming a sawed-off double-barrel shotgun at Red's head. Red's hand slowly moved away from his forty-five while he silently cursed himself for being so easily bushwhacked.

Bill, the buffalo hunter, chortled and slapped a greasy, fat thigh. "I swear now, if that ain't the funniest thang I ever seen?" He worked the tobacco around from one cheek to the other. "Tell you whut, feller. Why don't you throw that there pistol you got stuck under your coattails down on the rug, hum? Then Pete won't have to go wakin' up ever'body in the hotel. That ol' scatter-gun of hissen makes a powerful racket."

Red's jaws knotted. He took out the gun and threw it on the floor at the buffalo hunter's feet.

Billy picked up the gun and admired it. "My, that's purty. Looks bran' new. You Texas fellers sure got th' purty guns." He stuck it under his greasy buckskin jacket.

Red could hear the voices in Kalinec's room, muffled by the door. He heard the sharp smack of a man's fist against soft flesh, heard Celeste cry out, and then her sobs.

Sweat drenched his shirt. "Listen, he's going to kill that girl," Red said, his voice breaking. "You have to let me stop him—"

"Aw, it ain't seemly to go bustin' in on a private family fuss," the buffalo hunter said. "'Sides, me 'n

Pete here figured mebbe you'd like to go take a leetle ride with us in thet fancy buggy you got parked behind the hotel. I ain't been for a buggy ride in a heck of a long time."

Celeste screamed in the room. Red threw himself blindly at the door. The big man grabbed him. For a second they struggled silently. The buffalo hunter was as strong as a bull. But Red was taller by two inches, and twenty years of fighting the brush country had given him wide shoulders and muscles of steel. As frantic as he was, he probably could have knocked the big man over, but the half-breed Indian came running across the hall and smashed the stock of the sawed-off twelve-gauge against the back of his head and his knees buckled.

Dazed, Red was only dimly conscious of the two men dragging him down a side stairway and out the back door to the buggy. Pain jolted down his spine as the wheels jogged over ruts on the way out of town. The night air helped clear his head. He was wedged between Billy and the Indian.

"I swear, this is a purty leetle rig," Billy said happily. His lips smacked wetly as he chewed, and he hummed tunelessly.

They rode out of town a short distance and then Billy stopped the rig and pulled Red out.

"See, feller, this ain't nothin' personal," he said. "I like you Texas fellers, but a man pays me to do a job, I got to give him his money's worth."

The Indian pinned Red's arms behind him. Billy

came up to him, grinning, his hair standing up in red tufts in the moonlight and brown tobacco juice sluicing down his chin. He swung his huge paws, slapping Red's head from side to side like a bear cuffing him. And then he drove his fists into Red's stomach. Pain doubled Red in a blinding sheet. He heard his ribs crack. He gasped for breath. The ground came up and hit him in the face. Then Billy kicked him. Both men worked him over on the ground, kicking and hitting him. A great black void sucked Red down.

Some cowmen riding into town early the next morning found him half-unconscious on the side of the road. They picked him up and carried him to the deputy sheriff. They put him on a bunk in an empty cell and called the doctor. He applied bandages and liniment, grumbling at being awakened needlessly at such an early hour. "Hell, you can't permanently damage these Texas brush poppers," he muttered.

The deputy sent word out to the Lazy R camp. Thirty-Thirty and some of his riders came into town to take Red out to the camp. By then talk about the trouble between Red Martinue and Leslie Kalinec over Kalinec's beautiful wife, Celeste, had spread through town, so by the time Red felt like talking, Thirty-Thirty already knew all about it.

"I don't like it," Thirty-Thirty said darkly. "Messin' with a woman that carries another man's brand. That's bad business, Red. Woman like that ain't nothin' but trouble."

"Leave me alone, Pa," Red said, holding his head.

Thirty-Thirty shook his head. "That's somethin' I never done, messed with a branded heifer. You want to have some fun, there's plenty of single women in Dodge."

"Pa, I'm big enough to know what I'm doing. You don't know anything about Celeste."

Thirty-Thirty looked angry, but he dropped the argument.

For the next two days there was an air of quiet tension around the Lazy R camp. Manuel and his *vaqueros* cleaned their guns and sharpened their knives. After forty-eight hours Red was able to ride again. Late that afternoon, the men of the Lazy R saddled their horses and rode slowly into Dodge, in a body. Thirty-Thirty, Red, and Manuel rode up front, all of them quiet. The setting sun glinted on their guns, strapped low on their thighs and loose in the scabbards.

When they rode into the streets of Dodge, men looked at them and moved out of sight, off the sidewalks and away from the open doors of buildings. The stepping of the horse drove pain through Red's bruised, stiff body, and made his cracked ribs grate. But the anger in him was bigger than the soreness of his body.

They tied the horses at the hitch rails in the center of town and the *vaqueros* helped Red down from the saddle because he was too stiff to do it alone. He walked into the nearest saloon, looked over the crowd, then came out and went to the next one, the Lazy R men following him. When they came to the Dead Meskin saloon, Red looked inside and nodded to the others and they slowly filed inside, scuffing the floor with their boot heels and jangling spurs.

The bartender looked at their faces, quickly poured their drinks and got out from behind the bar. Red looked over his whisky at the back-bar mirror that Thirty-Thirty had shattered a few nights ago. Boards had been nailed across the cracked glass to hold it in place until a new mirror arrived by train from St. Louis. Red could see his face, distorted by the cracks in the mirror, but even more by the swollen bruises and cuts.

He swallowed his whisky and turned around with the bitter taste of anger rising in his throat.

Across the room Billy, the huge buffalo hunter, and his friend, the half-breed Pete, were sitting at a card table with a group of buffalo hunters. Their card game had frozen in mid-play. Billy sat with a forgotten drink in one hand, staring at Red and the Lazy R men at the bar. A smile was frozen on his lips and he'd forgotten the tobacco stuffed in one cheek and brown juice trickled unnoticed down his chin.

"I guess we got a little business to finish, ain't we, mister?" Red asked.

Billy smiled at him, but his blue eyes darted about and he licked at the corner of his mouth. His red hair was standing up in uncombed patches and his buck-skin looked even greasier than before.

"Aw, I don't want no trouble." He grinned. "You got half of Texas with you."

"They just come along to see your *amigo* Pete don't go bustin' me back of the head when I'm busy with you," Red said softly, pushing himself away from the bar and heading toward Billy.

The huge buffalo hunter sat there like a toad. He giggled as Red moved toward him. He put his drink down and wiped the back of his hand across his mouth. His blue eyes looked at his friends at the table, and then back at Red. He rubbed his hand through his wiry red hair.

Behind him, the half-breed was easing his hand toward his sawed-off shotgun propped against one table leg. He got his hand on it, when a Lazy R *vaquero* at the bar shot him in the shoulder and he tumbled out of his chair, upsetting the table. Guns and knives were suddenly bristling in the hands of the other *vaqueros*, and the buffalo hunters moved away from the table, backing against a wall, careful to keep their hands away from their weapons.

Billy looked around, his lips set in a frozen grin. He stood up, like a huge bear, with his long, powerful arms dangling at his side, his hands flexing, his pale blue eyes wary and mean. He came lumbering toward Red, his hands reaching out. But Red stepped inside his grasp and before Billy could close his arms in a bone-crushing bear hug, Red's fist smashed his face and he sprawled back against a post, his crushed nose spurting blood.

Billy yanked a Bowie knife out of his belt and lunged at Red, the breath wheezing through his grinning lips. But Red sidestepped fast as a brush jack rabbit and the knife slid three inches into the pine-board wall. Before

Billy could jerk it free, Red's fist sank into his belly. It was like hitting a barrel, but it drove the wind out of the big man and his face turned purple.

Red hit him again and again. Every time his fist drummed the huge man's barrel torso, or smashed into his face, savage satisfaction jolted up Red's arms. Billy was no boxer. He fought like a bear with brute strength, swinging his huge arms wildly, grabbing chairs and bottles. But Red dodged them and hit him again and again. Billy was groggy on his feet, his eyes dull with pain. His face was streaked with blood, his nose smashed out of shape, his still-grinning lips split and swollen. He staggered blindly, while Red stung him with crashing jabs and roundhouse swings.

Billy began walking in a circle, and then suddenly he went crashing to the floor like a huge tree falling. He sprawled out and lay still.

Red stood over him, breathing hard. The *vaqueros* gave a rousing cheer. They came to Red to slap his shoulder and offer him drinks of tequila. Thirty-Thirty poured whisky over his son's cut hands. "That was the best fight I ever seen," he roared. "That big feller come down like a tailed steer!"

They all had another drink on the house, since the bartender had run out, and then they went outside to their horses.

"Guess we kin head back to Texas now," Thirty-Thirty said heartily.

But Red shook his head. "I still got business at the hotel, Pa. This is personal. You go on."

Thirty-Thirty looked at his son angrily. "It's that no-count woman agin—"

"You ain't got no call to say that about her," Red snapped.

For a second the two Martinues glared at each other with the anger of two stubborn, headstrong men. Then Red turned on his heel.

He walked stiffly, still limping, down the street to the hotel. He went up the stairs straight to Kalinec's room. This time he was wearing the rough Levi's and dusty shirt of a trail cowhand, and a six-gun strapped low and handy on his right thigh.

He didn't bother to knock. He shook the doorknob and when it didn't open, he kicked the knob in with his heel.

The door flew inward. The room was in shadows, with only one small lamp on the table. Kalinec was not there. Celeste was alone in the room, on the bed. She was sitting up, staring with wide-eyed fright at him, holding a sheet to cover her nakedness.

Red took a step toward the bed and then his face turned pale. "My God—" he whispered.

There was an angry purple bruise above Celeste's left eyebrow. But Kalinec had not concentrated on her face. It was her back that had taken most of the beating. Raw, bloody streaks crisscrossed it from her neck to her hips. He had used a quirt on her. That was why she was in bed unclothed. She couldn't even bear the touch of cloth on her body.

Red found some salve and gently treated the wounds

while she rested her forehead against his shoulder and cried brokenly. "He's kept me locked in here since—since that night," she whimpered. "He wouldn't even let a doctor in."

"You're going away with me tonight," Red told her. "He won't hurt you again. I'm taking you back to Texas with me. Do you think you can ride?"

She nodded, pressing her tearful face against his arm. "I'll do anything to get away from him. I was so afraid you'd never come back—" she whispered.

He turned his back while she dressed and filled a small bag with clothes. Her face was pale, but she smiled when he turned around. "I'll be all right," she said.

They left the hotel together and Red helped her up in front of him in the saddle. "We won't travel far at first. Not until you feel stronger."

When Red brought Celeste into camp that night, Thirty-Thirty's face turned dark with anger. He walked away from them to the edge of camp. Red made a bed for her in one of the cook wagons. Later, he went to look for his father.

"I don't want that furrin' French woman goin' back with us," Thirty-Thirty told Red flatly.

Red's young jaw knotted stubbornly. "Well, she's goin'."

"Listen, son," Thirty-Thirty said, "you listen to your pa, now. I'm a sight older than you. People back home don't think much about a man that's a wife-stealer."

"Pa, you're talkin' *loco*," Red said angrily. "That

girl's husband is a maniac. He almost killed her. He used a whip on her, Pa." Tears came into his eyes, telling about it.

Thirty-Thirty shook his head. "Other people don't know about that part. They'll just say you stole another man's wife. I want you to find a good woman, son. One day you're goin' to be one of the biggest cattlemen in Texas. Maybe you'll go to the Legislature in Austin. You want a wife that's respected, that will help you. That girl"—he jerked a thumb toward the cook wagon—"whut kind of rancher's wife will she make? Whut will the sun and brush do to that pale skin of hers? She's too pretty to want to live on a brush ranch. Her kind has to have city lights and men to look at her admirin'—"

"Pa, you've got all them big ideas about makin' the Lazy R the biggest ranch in Texas. It's still just a little spread. Maybe it will be big someday, maybe not. I don't aim to pick a woman to fit that danged ranch!"

Thirty-Thirty glared at his son. "I've fought that brush to start a place for you an' my gran'-children an' it don't mean no more to you than that," he said bitterly. "All right, if you don't care nothin' about your land, jest remember this. That woman's husband ain't goin' to know any rest until he puts a bullet between your shoulder blades. From now on, until he kills you, or you kill him, you'll never have a night's peace. Every time you ride into some town, you'll wonder if the next minute a bullet will come out of an alley. You got a man on your trail now, son...."

CHAPTER TWELVE

They went back to Texas. There were slow weeks of long trails made hot by the sun. And the drenching rain that drove against a man's face and trickled down the neck under his slicker. The streams were dry and they were swollen, depending on where you were, north of the Red River or south.

At first Celeste had to be taken in the cook wagon, slow because she was feverish with pain, and the jolting made her clutch the bedclothes of the rough pallet in her fists. But the raw streaks gradually healed, leaving faint white markings on her back, and the bruises turned from purple to yellow, and her broken ribs healed. Then she rode with the men. "I grew up in the west, I told you," she insisted to Red. But she was still a woman and not up to a man's pace in the saddle.

Red rode beside her during the day. At night he spread his bedroll near the cook wagon where she slept. He slept with his hand on his gun and during the day while they rode, he turned often to look back, scanning the prairie for sign of a rider who might be following them. Kalinec would be crazy to follow them now. The *vaqueros* surrounded them. He would follow them eventually, trailing them with information he could get from the cattle buyers in Dodge who knew of the home of the Lazy R. But surely not now. Still, Red looked back, and slept with his hand on his gun.

And he rode close to Celeste, looking at her during the long ride across the rivers and the prairies that stretched to nowhere. Her face glistened with sweat in the sun and dust caked at the corners of her mouth. Rain drove against their ponchos, matting her hair and making her shiver. She wore a pair of Red's Levi's, rolled up, and an old shirt that became torn and stiff with mud.

The saddles rubbed and the horses' manes brushed their hands. They smelled the horse sweat. Bacon fried as dawn winds blew sand on the prairie and rolled tumble weeds against them. And a horse broke his leg in a prairie dog hole and they shot him and rode on. A *vaquero* took his guitar from his back and sang as he rode, his body bowed in the saddle under the heat and the clouds with the rain and the buzzards and dust storms that choked and blinded.

The rains came at night, putting out the hissing campfire and the horses whinnied, afraid of the lightning. A gully washer. The prairie turned into a lake. Boiling streams formed on flat ground, eating at the dirt. The men crouched in their ponchos against bushes and small hummocks for shelter in their misery. The canvas over the cook tent, rotten from the sun and dust and weather, split apart.

Celeste put on a poncho, already soaked though.

The rain slashed and thunder shook the ground and she shivered, afraid. The wagon was on a flatrock bed and she crawled under the wagon for shelter.

Red plowed into the driving rain, his head down. He searched the ruined cook wagon for her and she called to him from under the bed, looking up at him through the spokes of the wheel. He followed her under the wagon, and put his arm around her and they sat with their wet faces close.

Her face had been blistered by the sun. Her lips were cracked. The rain glued her matted hair to her neck. But he looked at her and she was beautiful. He kissed her, finding her wet mouth in the darkness.

He talked into her ear, above the thunder and the driving cloudburst. "Only a little more of this and we'll be home." She nodded, pressing her cheek against his.

The wind shook the wagon above them and the rain drove at them through the spokes of the wagon. "Celeste," he whispered, "I want you so much—"

Her arms around him tightened. "It's all right," she whispered against the rain. She kissed him, moaning softly. "Oh, Red—"

"As soon as we get back I'll see a lawyer in San Antonio about gettin' you a divorce," he said against the rain. "I want to marry you, Celeste."

Her eyes clouded and she turned her face away. "Please don't talk about it," she said in a small voice. "You don't know me, Red. Please don't talk about marrying me—"

The rain drove through the spokes and hissed at

them. He wouldn't listen to her. "I love you," he said.

She closed her eyes tightly and the rain on her face mingled with the salt of her tears. "Please don't talk about it—"

The wind blew her words away, into the rain, and he held her close through the night-long storm.

The next day they rode through the mud. Thirty-Thirty was a solitary figure, riding apart from his son, his eyes angry and brooding. A lonely, craggy old mesquite tree, whipped and toughened by the years, and bent doggedly into the wind. He hadn't exchanged a dozen words with Red since they left Dodge City. When they came to the rolling plains of south Texas, he raised his brooding eyes. They glowered from the dark shadow of his hat brim. The girl rode into brush with the other men. He didn't look at her. He had refused to speak to her.

Red left Celeste at a respectable boarding house in Cherokee Flats and sun-blistered, dirty, bone-weary, she looked at a real bed for the first time in weeks.

Red continued on to the Lazy R with Thirty-Thirty and the *vaqueros* to see that the house was ready and a barbecue started for her visit on the week end.

In the town the talk had already started about the woman Red Martinue had brought back with him from Dodge City. They talked about her beauty and some whispered that she still wore a wedding ring, and as Thirty-Thirty had warned his son, most of the talk was not kind.

On Saturday Red returned to town, wearing the new

suit he had bought in Dodge City. He left his horse at the livery stable and rented a buggy for the ride back to the ranch. When Celeste came out on the porch of the rooming house she was wearing a pink cotton dress and carrying a frilly parasol. Red stood looking at her, the girl who had worn Levi's and forded streams and huddled against dust storms with him and lay in his arms under a wet wagon through a night-long drizzle.

She smiled, then pouted. "I wanted to look pretty for you. But the stores here don't have any clothes for women. Ugly old cotton dresses and bonnets! This parasol was the only pretty thing I could find and the store owner had it hidden under his counter. Do you think I'll be branded a loose woman for carrying it in public?" She giggled.

They walked out to the buggy and slowly rode down the main street. Celeste sat close to him and tucked her hand in his arm and looked up at him with teasing eyes. His ears turned red. He felt the staring eyes from the people on the walks.

They neared the middle of town and Red nodded toward one of the saloons. "That's the Red Lantern— place I told you about where I was born."

She stared at it, fascinated.

Cherokee Flats had spread out and built up in the more than twenty years since Red was born in the Red Lantern saloon. The tents and lean-tos of the settlement had given way to substantial frame buildings with false fronts. There was a dry goods store, livery stable, hardware store, blacksmith shops, several saloons, and a two-story hotel.

It was the largest town in the ranching country of the brush wilderness of south Texas. The main road from San Antonio to Brownsville cut through Cherokee Flats and the stagecoach stopped for an overnight rest at the hotel.

They followed the main street to the end and took the dirt road that wound out into the brush. The brush thickets closed them off into a strange and terrifying world. After they had ridden for a while, Red told her, "This is Lazy R land. As far as you can see to the east and west from here is ours. There's the open range too, most of the brush country now, but my pa says to get deeds because one day there'll be fences around what belongs to a man and what don't. I don't reckon I'll see it in my lifetime, but I guess it's good to have a deed and know that you got rangeland nobody can cut you out of with a fence. The biggest ranch here is the Boxed X off to the west. They own a whole passel of land, bought off Mexicans who had the original Spanish grant deeds. They're fighting to keep us off the open range and buying up all they can so there'll be a time when they own all of the *brasada*. That's what Thirty-Thirty says. One day either the Boxed X or the Lazy R will own all this with a fence around it, and the other one will be out of business."

Celeste stared wide-eyed at the fierce thickets that rose up around them like fortresses of thorns. There was wild, untamed beauty among the thorns, the waxy red and yellow berries, the shower-of-gold flowers, the purple cactus blooms. Red pointed out the bushes and thorny trees, old friends he had known since childhood who sometimes tried to scratch his eyes out. He called them by their Spanish and Indian names, the only ones he knew. He told her about the coma that had thorns like the rest, but also had a sweet blue berry that fed the Mexican doves.

He told her of the fierce junco, the leafless all-thorn. And of the legend of the Mexican people, that Christ's crown of thorns had been made of it. Birds would not light in it except the butcher bird, a killer who cruelly speared insects and lizards on the thorns, returning for them when the sun had dried them. Celeste listened to the story and shuddered.

But there were things that a man learned about the monte and it lost some of its terror. The bitter, sharp armagosa brewed a medicinal tea. Prickly pear made a poultice that healed thorn stabs. Fruit of the agrito made a ruby-colored jelly with a wild tang. The Spanish dagger jabbed into the flesh carried a poison that counteracted the venom of a rattlesnake bite. Tea brewed from the huisache bark could heal the internal bruises of a man knocked from his horse by the limbs. Red told her of these things.

They came to the ranch clearing with its buildings of frame and adobe and its corrals of mesquite limbs. The *vaqueros* bowed polite greetings to Celeste. But Thirty-Thirty threw a saddle on his horse and rode into the brush.

The Mexican woman who kept house had prepared

the extra room in the big house for Celeste. At sunset they ate barbecue under the gnarled mesquite trees in the yard. The ranch hands had buried the *cabrita* in the ground with mesquite coals for twenty-four hours. Tender, barbecued *cabrita*. And pinto beans, mashed and fried the Mexican way, and crisp tacos and steaming pots of coffee.

Then, when it was dark, a *baile*. Lanterns were hung in the trees. Three *vaqueros* made an orchestra with a guitar, fiddle, and a bass contrived from a broom stick, washtub and length of rope. They danced with their *señoritas* on the patio under the trees. Celeste watched them and her eyes sparkled and she clapped her hands and laughed gaily.

Later, Red strolled with her to the shadows of the porch. "This will be your home as soon as we're married. One day it'll be a big ranch. I'll work hard to make it what you want."

He tried to take her into his arms, but she turned away. She gazed at the black wall of the monte surrounding them on four sides. Moonlight tipped the thorns with silver. A shiver suddenly ran through her body. She knew that Leslie Kalinec would be following them.

CHAPTER THIRTEEN

Monday morning the man in the black suit stood at his hotel window in the second story of the Cherokee Flats hotel, watching the horses and buckboards that came into town. After a while his gaze fell on a buggy coming into main street from the south. It was the buggy Red Martinue was driving, bringing Celeste back into town after the week-end visit at the ranch. The man checked his forty-five for the final time, shoved it into his belt, and walked downstairs.

Red left Celeste at the boarding house with the promise, "Wednesday, we're goin' to take the stage to San Antonio and see about that lawyer." Then he got back in the buggy to return it to the livery stable.

Celeste could have stayed on at the ranch, but Red didn't want to make talk any worse than it already was, and cheapen the girl he loved in the eyes of his community. As it was, it would be a long time before his neighbors accepted her. When he brought her out to the ranch to live, it would be as his wife.

In the boarding house the landlady, Mrs. Fulton, trailed Celeste to her room. "Man come by here lookin' for you Sunday mornin'," she said, wiping her hands on her apron. "Said he'd asked around town and heard you had a room here. Wouldn't leave no message. Stranger, I reckon, at least I never seen him around here before—"

Celeste spun about. She stared at the landlady with frightened eyes. Then she caught up her skirt and ran out of the house, leaving a startled Mrs. Fulton behind.

Red drove the buggy into the stable and waited for the owner to saddle the horse he had left. He leaned against the open door of the livery stable and rolled a cigarette. Across the street, a man in a dark suit stepped down from the boardwalk and moved toward the stable, but Red hardly noticed him. His mind was filled with Celeste and plans for the future. He had his mind made up to fix up the ranch house so Celeste would like to live there. It was all right for men the way it was, but a woman would like things nicer. They could see about the things she'd want for the house while they were in San Antonio and have them shipped down by freight cart.

The man came into the yard of the stable, walking slowly toward the open door where Red leaned, waiting for his horse. Red half drowsed in the morning sun as he lit his cigarette and thought about Celeste and the ranch and all the things he could do when she was his wife.

The town was still that early in the morning. Sparrows ran along the livery stable fence, chirping. A Mexican freight cart rumbled by out in the street. The metallic clang! of the blacksmith's hammer floated in the air.

The town drowsed in the early morning sunlight.

The man in the dark suit stopped a dozen yards away. He took his hand from under his coat and he was holding a gun. He said, "Red Martinue, look at me. I want to see your face when I kill you."

Leslie Kalinec had grown thin since he left Dodge City, weeks ago, riding to San Antonio, and then coming to Cherokee Flats by stage. The dark suit hung on him loosely. He was being consumed by a fever that ate at his body and his brain—the fever of jealous hate. It burned in his head; his cheeks were flushed with it and his eyes were sick with it.

His gun roared, shattering the stillness of the morning. A giant fist slammed Red against the stable wall, knocking his cigarette from his hand. He felt surprise and shock and numbness, but at first no pain. He stared at Kalinec, seeing him quite clearly, the heavy gold watch chain across his vest, the gun in his hand, still smoking. He could hear horses whinnying and kicking their stalls inside the stable, startled by the pistol shot.

It was a moment frozen in time. Then Kalinec's cheek twitched. His eyes, yellow with sick hate looked at Red and he lifted his gun for a second shot.

Then, past his shoulder, Red saw Celeste, running from across the street, to the open gate of the livery stable yard. She was screaming his name and sobbing.

Kalinec whirled about. A spasm jerked his whole body as he faced the wife who had run away with Red Martinue.

Red gasped, "Celeste! Go back!" And then for the first time he realized that the bullet was in his chest and there was fire in his lungs and blood in his throat.

But Celeste was already inside the yard. She stood frozen, her fingers reaching for her lips. Her wide, terror-stricken gaze was fastened on Kalinec.

"He's crazy—he'll kill you!" Red cried hoarsely.

Kalinec was already aiming his gun at Celeste. She could only stand there helpless, staring at him.

Drops of sweat ran down Kalinec's face. A chill shook him from head to foot. "You and your lover will sleep in hell tonight!" he screamed in a high-pitched voice. Then his finger tightened on the trigger.

Every breath Red drew now smashed pain through him. A cold sweat filmed his face. Darkness was closing the perimeter of his vision. The objects he could still see were becoming blurred. With all his will he clutched at his fading consciousness. He drew his gun fast. His bullet spun Kalinec around.

A look of surprise crossed Kalinec's face. For a second he blinked at the man who had shot him. Then his gun roared. Splinters crashed from the stable wall inches from Red's ear.

Red squeezed his trigger again. His second shot kicked Leslie Kalinec backward. He fell to one knee. He was blinking, dazed and befuddled. He worked to raise his gun again, his lips skinned back from his clenched teeth. But Red fired first and Kalinec sprawled on his back, his gun skidding out of his hand.

Then Red's forty-five became unbearably heavy. It

spilled from his numb fingers. Through the haze he could see Celeste running toward him, but she seemed to grow smaller and fade away. The curtain of darkness closed off his vision altogether. Faintly, from a great distance, he heard Celeste sobbing his name. Then even that faded and he heard no more....

By the time the echo of the last shot had faded, a crowd began gathering at the scene of the shooting. They carried Red to Doctor King's office, leaving a trail of blood in the dusty street the entire way. The doctor probed for the bullet lodged high in the right side of Red's chest, packed the wound with dressing to slow the bleeding, and covered him with a blanket to lessen the shock. Then he said, shaking his head, "The rest is up to God, and we better pray He's on our side today."

Celeste huddled on a couch outside the room where the doctor was fighting to save Red's life. She was sobbing wretchedly.

They got word to Thirty-Thirty out in the brush and he rode into town stiff-faced. When he strode into the doctor's office, his gaze fell on Celeste, and his eyes burned darkly. "You brought this trouble on my son," he said.

CHAPTER FOURTEEN

Red walked through a dark valley. A void and darkness without time or space was above and below. And before it a greater distance and a force sweeping him there and he felt no resistance and no desire to go back. No sensation, no pain. The quietness and peaceful safety of the distance called him and he wanted to go there. But there was a struggle. Daylight came back in snatches and the pain and bother of existence with it and he irritably pushed it away, longing again for the peace of the great depths that offered him surcease. He was so weary and there was rest out there. But Celeste called to him and her hands touched him, pleading for him to come back. He wanted her to leave him alone because his longing for the peace was more than for her. He didn't want to remember her. But her tears fell on him. The milky fog moved across the darkness. Through it, faintly, he could see her face. The large, dark eyes. The fair skin. The sweet red mouth that trembled and the white throat that curved to its secret hollow.

He wanted to reach up and touch her cheek, but his hand was too heavy. "I'm so weak I can't touch you," he whispered in surprise and it was the first thing he'd said in days.

Tears ran down her cheeks to the corner of her smile. "Then you must get strong again, *mon chéri*, so you can touch me."

"Oh, I'll get strong for that—" he whispered, and then slept peacefully and the dark winds faded and passed away.

She stayed by his side day and night, nursing him, feeding him with a spoon, bathing him. When he could be moved to the ranch, she came along to care for him, staying in the spare room of the big house. Dark anger burned in Thirty-Thirty's eyes when he looked at her, but his son's will was as strong as his, and Celeste stayed.

In the afternoons Celeste read aloud from a book to pass the time while Red convalesced. Those afternoons, the ranch was very quiet. All the hands were out in the brush working cattle. The Mexican housekeeper was taking her siesta. It was the first time since they'd left Dodge city that Red and the girl were entirely alone.

She wore a thin cotton dress that clung to the curves of her healthy young body. Her hair was piled on top of her head for coolness, leaving the damp curve of her neck bare as she bent over the book. There was a faint sheen of perspiration on her face and the waist of her dress was damp, clinging to her body.

Once she looked up as she turned a page and pressed her lips together reprovingly. "Red Martinue, you're not listening to a word I've been reading!"

"That's right. Sometimes a man'd rather look than listen if he's got something to look at. Come here."

She shook her head. "No!" But her eyes teased him. "Oh, all right then—"

She put down the book and sat on the edge of his bed and smiled at him. He held her hand. "Sometimes I can't stop looking at you."

"I look so awful though," she sighed. "This heat!" She wiped the perspiration from her forehead with the curved flat of her palms.

"You're beautiful," he said. "I don't care how hot it is." Then he said slowly, "Celeste?"

"Yes, *mon chéri.*"

"That sure is a pretty word. I never heard it before, but it's kinda like music when you say it. What does it mean?"

"What, '*mon chéri*'?" She laughed softly. "It's a French word my mother taught me. She used to call me that when she was happy. It means 'my sweet' or 'my darling,' or however you'd say it in English."

"I guess you only say it to somebody you love—"

"Now, I didn't say that! You could say it to a good friend, or a kitten," she teased him.

He looked at her beautiful white hand, touching the fingers and the ovals of her nails with his big, stubby brown fingers. "Celeste, there's somethin' I've been wantin' to ask you about. It's—well, it ain't easy, though. It's about Leslie Kalinec—"

Her face sobered. She looked down at the sheet, smoothing it with her fingers. "What about him?" she whispered through stiff lips.

"Well—" Red hesitated. "This ain't easy to say, but I have to talk to you about it. I mean, you were his wife for four or five years and—well, were you in love with him any more at all?"

She bit her lip, looking down at the sheet. "Oh, Red, I don't think I was ever in love with him at all, in the way you mean. I was a child when we married. He was—well, more of a father to me at first. Then when he lost everything, this sickness came into his mind and I—I was afraid of him—"

"But living with him, being with him all the time, his wife. And then I killed him. I have to know how you feel toward me about that. Celeste, I'm the man who killed your husband."

Her face paled and her fingers trembled. "Please don't say it that way."

"But it's true."

"It's not true—not like that. He was a crazy man. He would have killed us both. What choice did you have?" She drew a deep breath, then looked into his eyes. "Red, I have to tell you this. I went out to the cemetery when he was buried. It was the only time I left your side, even for a moment. But I had to go and I knew you'd understand. It was such a lonely, bleak cemetery, out there on the edge of town, with the grass all dry and burned from the heat and no flowers at all. No one else was there except the men who dug the grave and lowered the coffin into the ground and the preacher that I'd asked to come and say a few words and—and myself.

"I cried when they lowered the coffin into the ground with the ropes. But I cried because it was such a lonely place and death is such a lonely thing. I cried because Leslie was a sick man, all twisted in his mind. I had been afraid of him for a long time and I'd even hated him the way you hate something you fear. But you can cry for someone who is sick and tortured.

"Do you see what I'm trying to tell you? I tried to cry because he had been my husband and he was dead now. But I couldn't cry for that reason. The tears wouldn't come. I could only cry because life is such a sad thing sometimes, and so terrifying. Now do you understand, *mon chéri*?"

The room was quiet in the stillness of the midday heat. Red brought her fingers to his lips, pressing them gently. "I understand. And I feel better. I know it wasn't an easy thing to talk about, but it was something that had to be said. Because I love you, Celeste, and I want to marry you." He looked up into her eyes. "And now there's no reason why we can't be married in a few weeks, as soon as I'm back on my feet."

She turned her face away, not answering.

"Celeste?"

"Oh, Red, I—I don't know—"

"What do you mean, you don't know?"

"I—I guess I mean I'm afraid."

"Of what, for heaven's sake?"

"Of marriage. Of myself. Of—of, I don't know! Mostly I'm afraid of making you unhappy, I suppose," she cried.

"Now that makes a heck of a lot of sense! I love you. How can you make a feller that loves you unhappy by gettin' married to him?"

She bit her lip. "Oh, Red, you don't know me very well!"

"Don't know you? Didn't I ride beside you all the way back from Dodge? Haven't you been with me day and night since I was shot?"

She shook her head. "That's not really knowing anybody. You're in love with me, Red. You see only the good things. Sometimes I—I don't think I know myself very well. Sometimes I think there is another girl inside me, just a shadow at times and very real at others, so real she becomes me. I'm ashamed of her, because she is greedy and selfish. I think my mother put her there, and taught her to hate being poor the way we were, and to want nice things, and wealth and power. She'll never let me be content with the simple home and family that satisfy others, this other person inside me. Do you understand at all what I'm trying to tell you, Red?"

"But you'll have money! Someday the Lazy R will be a big ranch, the biggest ranch between the Nueces and the Rio Grande. Someday you'll be the wife of one of the biggest ranchers in Texas. You'll have every-thing—"

"Someday—" she whispered sadly. "It's such a beautiful dream, Red. My father was a dreamer. That's all my life has ever been to me so far—a dream.

Perhaps like you say one day your ranch will be big and wealthy, but now it's only a small struggling ranch in a god-forsaken country of heat and brush. I—I just don't know if I can be a rancher's wife. Maybe this will all just be a dream too—"

"I'll make it real," Red promised. "Trust me—"

He pulled her closer, his big hands going around her waist. She spread her hands against his broad chest, resisting him. "Red, you mustn't," she whispered.

He kissed her, holding her very close, his arms growing strong.

"Oh, Red," she whispered. "Please—you'll hurt your wound. You're not strong enough—"

He kissed her again and his arms were so tight around her she couldn't breath. "Not strong enough?" he grinned.

Her lovely face was flushed and she breathed swiftly when he released her. "Oh, Red, I do love you and want you."

Three weeks later they were married in the yard of the Lazy R under the mesquite trees. The circuit riding parson who was holding a revival in town performed the ceremony. All the *vaqueros* were present, their boots polished to the glow of rich old mahogany, wearing their finest regalia—tight black trousers with ornately stitched pockets and fancy filigree trim down the sides, shirts with silver studding and silver spurs, and the huge sombreros of Old Mexico. Neighbors came, mostly out of respect for the Martinues, but the women did not speak to Celeste and the men looked at her and grinned at one another self-consciously.

Friends, neighbors, businessmen from town, *vaqueros*, they were all at Red Martinue's wedding. But Thirty-Thirty was not there. He was in town getting drunk by himself.

There was a three-day fiesta with barbecues, horse racing, game cock fights, and a *baile* every night. The ranch yard was filled with the wagons, buckboards, and horses of neighbors who had come from as far as fifty miles and stayed for the entire three days. There were people sleeping in the ranch house, bunk house, in wagons, under the barn, in corrals.

They barbecued whole steers over smoldering mesquite coals and cooked *cabrita*. They baked turkeys in pits in the ground, heating the pit with coals, then burying the turkey, feathers and all in the pit, and building a fire over the covering. After twenty hours they lifted the turkey out and the skin and feathers slid off of their own weight, and the meat was so juicy and tender it melted on the tongue. The women brought hundreds of pies, and Red had whisky carted from town by the barrel.

They danced at night and bet on the horse races and game cock fights during the day and wrestled on the ground and broke wild horses and tailed steers for sport.

Doctor King closed his office in town and stayed at the ranch for the three-day celebration, knowing full well he'd have no rest anyway. He set three broken collarbones, took seventeen stitches in a *vaquero* who got in a knife fight, diagnosed two cases of measles among the kids, and helped deliver a calf behind the barn.

There were three fist fights and one stabbing, but everything happened in the spirit of the occasion and nobody left with hard feelings.

Red and Celeste stole away on the morning of the second day and took the stagecoach into San Antonio for their honeymoon. Red had mended completely, except for a little stiffness. He was filled with complete happiness. His chest swelled with pride when they walked down Houston street and people turned to look at his beautiful bride. He felt ten feet tall.

"I'm going to give you everything you ever wanted," he promised Celeste. "I'm goin' to build the Lazy R into the biggest ranch in Texas, just like Thirty-Thirty always dreamed, and we'll take that danged Boxed X ranch and ram it down Duncan Zepeda's throat. I'm goin' to make you one of the richest wives in Texas!"

They stayed at a hotel on Alamo Plaza and walked along the river and listened to the strumming of Mexican guitars in the evening breeze. And nothing could have been more beautiful.

But when they returned from the honeymoon, hard times were facing the Lazy R. Its days were numbered.

CHAPTER FIFTEEN

They made one more successful cattle drive to Kansas the following spring. But that year the markets were oversupplied. Vast herds had to be held over on the Kansas and Nebraska prairies the next winter, and in the severe cold cattle froze to death by the hundreds of thousands. The following year, 1873, was the year of the great financial panic. Nearly all the banks in Kansas City closed their doors. Beef retailed in Kansas City for two and a half cents a pound. Cattlemen of southwest Texas, starting their cattle drives north, were warned there would be no markets, and they had to turn back.

Hard times fell on the ranchmen of Texas. Money was scarce and cattle almost worthless, but for the value in their hides and tallow. Instead of being branded and driven to market, they were slaughtered on the prairies. The beef was left to the buzzards and coyotes and the hide was sold for the few cents it would bring.

The range war of long standing between the Boxed X and the Lazy R became a skinning war. Riders of both ranches would kill cattle on the range, regardless of the brand they carried, skin the hides, and leave the carcasses to rot. In the cold, wet northers of winter, the cattle drifted south toward the coast by the thousands across the unfenced prairie and they banked up along bayous and creeks and bogged down and died. Those that didn't freeze were killed and all of them were stripped of their hides. There were acres of blotted, rotting carcasses.

The bitter feud between the Zepedas and the Martinues smoldered into fresh anger in the year of the skinning war, and three of the Lazy R *vaqueros* lost their lives that year, shot by Boxed X bushwhackers as they rode in the brush. Josiah Zepeda had suffered a stroke and would spend the rest of his life in a chair. Duncan had taken over the running of the ranch and he pushed the range war with even more bitterness than his father had.

Thirty-Thirty grew gaunt and silent and his eyes glowed from the black shadows of his hat brim. He and Red stayed in the saddle until they came home and fell across the bed with their clothes on in dead exhaustion and after a few hours they would drag themselves out again, working just to hold onto the ranch, to pay the hands. But every month they had to let men go until there was just Manuel Vera and a handful of men.

Red lived through those days with defeat heavy on his shoulders and shame in his heart when he looked at Celeste. All his big promises! They would go to San Antonio every month to the opera house. They would take a steamship to New Orleans so she could buy the finest dresses from Paris as befitted the wife of a Texas cattle baron. All these things he had promised her and he had given her only a ranch house in the brush, baked by heat and stung by drought. He had not given her a new dress in a year. She was withdrawn and her dark eyes were brooding and rebellious when she stood on the porch staring at her prison walls of thorns. She was half-sick from the heat.

Late at night in the darkness after they had gone to bed they talked about what to do. The cattle business was dead. They talked about giving in to the Zepedas and selling the ranch. Celeste wanted very much to move into town. Red could put the money he'd get for the ranch into business, an overland freighting line or a meat packery on the coast, or a saloon.

It would be worse than cutting off his arm, to give up the Lazy R empire that was to have one day stretched the length of the vast brush land of south Texas. But he was bone-weary and discouraged and desperate. He was failing Celeste and her love for him would surely die, killed by the futility of this kind of life.

The last straw carne the day Thirty-Thirty rode out of the brush to the ranchyard, reeling in the saddle, his scalp split open by a bushwhacker's bullet, and sprawled to the ground. When Red helped carry the old man into the house, his mind was made up that he'd had enough of the righting and killing over dry brush and cattle that had become worthless. Thirty-Thirty had missed being killed by an inch. The very next time he rode out into the brush, he might not be so lucky. Red waited until the old man's scalp wound had healed and he was back on his feet. Then he quietly loaded some things into the buckboard and took Celeste into town and got them a room at the hotel. And he knew he'd never go back to the Lazy R again.

He sent word to Josiah Zepeda that he wanted to talk about selling out his half of the Lazy R, and then he waited. Although Zepeda could no longer ride a horse and had to be carried in a chair by two strong men, he still came into town to his bank several times a week and ran all his business ventures with a clear head. Red did not expect the Zepedas to reply immediately to his offer, no matter how surprised or elated they might be, because that was no way to do business. They let several days pass and then a message was delivered to Red at the hotel that if he wished to discuss a business transaction with Zepeda, he could come to his office at the bank.

But Red sent a note in reply by the messenger that he would only discuss the matter at his own convenience in his own room at the hotel. And thereby he won the first parry, making the Zepedas come to meet him on his own ground.

They came the following day, Duncan Zepeda, a grown man now, an inch or two taller than Red, stockier, and roughly handsome except for the jagged white scar that pulled at his right cheek. He touched the scar unconsciously with a gloved finger, remembering the day in the brush, seven years ago, when Red's spur had put it there, and an old hate burned in his eyes.

Two husky black men carried Zepeda's chair up

the stairs and put him down in the room facing Red. Red was shocked by the change in the powerful south Texan. His hair was silver white, his face hollow and pale, and the shadow of death was in his eyes. His left hand shook with palsy and he held it still under the robe across his lap with his right hand. But his mind was clear and his eyes were as hard as quartz.

"What's all this nonsense about, boy?" Zepeda demanded irritably. "What are you tryin' to pull?"

"I told you what I wanted to talk about in the note I sent you."

"A man talks business in an office, not a hotel room with women around."

Celeste was standing near the window, her face pale and lovely as she watched the meeting of these strong men.

"This is pretty important to my wife. I reckon she's got a right to hear," Red said.

"Woman's got no place around business talk," Josiah Zepeda muttered.

But his son Duncan was staring at the girl, his eyes narrowed and searching, his blood moving quicker through his veins. He had heard the talk about the beautiful woman that Red Martinue had married, but no one had come close to describing her. There wasn't another woman like this in the whole state of Texas! He wiped the back of his gloved hand across his lips, unmasked desire for her thickening in his stare.

She saw him looking at her and her cheeks colored. Her hand moved to her throat and she tore her gaze away from him, looking at Red.

But Red was facing Josiah Zepeda, with the business they had come for hovering in the air between them. He had not seen the way that Duncan looked at his wife.

Josiah Zepeda's hard eyes stabbed at Red angrily. "What kind of fool you take me for, boy? A man could peel the hide off Thirty-Thirty Martinue in strips and he wouldn't part with an acre of his land. What's your game?"

The life-long hate between the men lay sullen and tense in the room with the heat of the day that burned on the tin roof above them and put sweat on their faces.

"You're right about my pa. But I own half the land and the cattle and the buildings on the Lazy R. If I take it in my head I want to get out of the cattle business and sell my half of the ranch, that's up to me. I'm twenty-two and legal-aged."

The air grew still between the two men. Zepeda tapped his thumbnail against his teeth. His eyes were half-closed, shielding the thoughts in them. "I reckon then if a man's thinking about selling his place, he's got an asking price in mind."

"I figure it's up to you to make an offer."

Their gazes met, each studying and testing the other, the old man with years of ruthless, shrewd trading experience, and the young man with the knowledge of having something the old man wanted more than any thing else in the world, and wanted it while there were still a few years left in his sick body.

Duncan stayed out of the talk. He ran the Boxed X now, but the old man still made the decisions in a matter like this. He listened with half an ear to the talk between the other two men, but he looked at Celeste with the hunger growing heavy and demanding in him. He came to the decision that this was a woman he was going to possess if he had to kill Red Martinue to get her.

Josiah Zepeda leaned back in his chair, resting his thumbnail against the ridge of a tooth. His eyes were half-closed, studying Red. He appeared to doze and minutes ticked away without a word being said. Then he named a figure.

Red went over and opened the door. "Reckon there's no use talkin' about it any more, then."

"Wait a minute, wait a minute," Zepeda snapped. "Listen, boy, you know land ain't worth nothin' these days—and cattle worth less."

"That's why I'm makin' the offer to you. You think if I had any choice I'd talk a trade with you? I'd rather sell my land to the worst Yankee carpetbagger that draws a breath. But I know nobody else has the money to buy land right now, so I have to put it up to you. It's more 'n brush land you're buyin' an' you damn well know it. For twenty years you've wanted to run the Lazy R out of the brush country. With my half, you'd own a strip of land cutting the *brasada* north to south, and twenty miles wide. You could fence it, legal, and cut Thirty-Thirty's remaining half off from all the open range west clear to the Rio Grande. That's worth plenty to you and we both know it."

Josiah Zepeda was a hard businessman and a deadly poker player. But in that moment he had trouble hiding the gleam of excitement in his eyes. The breath whistled between his teeth. "You're offerin' this without Thirty-Thirty's knowledge. He'd kill you, boy. He'd kill his own son—" Zepeda leaned forward. "You got clear deeds on this land?"

"All the way back to the Spanish grants."

Red took a bundle of deeds out of his shirt, wrapped in oiled skin. Over twenty-two years ago, starting with the day Red was born in the Red Lantern saloon, Thirty-Thirty had been buying up these deeds. Every time he dug cattle out of the brush and sold them, he put some of the money in land that he bought from settlers, from Mexicans, from the state, until the legal boundaries of his land could have held a small New England state. This bundle of papers was over twenty-two years of a man's life. Red's eyes blurred as he laid them before Zepeda.

Red knew before the meeting ever took place that he would get the price he wanted, because he knew the value of what he was offering to Zepeda. To a dying man like Josiah Zepeda, there was no longer a need for money or a taste for women. But to die with an empire spread before him for his son and his grandchildren to inherit, to see a lifetime battle finished to satisfaction—this gave ease to dying and tempted a man to spend far beyond the value of a thing for practical purposes.

All of this was done without Thirty-Thirty's knowledge. But when the papers were signed and legally recorded, and the payment deposited in Red's name in gold coin, and Red Martinue ceased to be half-owner of the Lazy R ranch, the word raced from mouth to mouth and spread even out into the brush. It reached Thirty-Thirty, carried by a *vaquero* who had returned from town with supplies.

Early the next morning the town of Cherokee Flats was roused by enraged bellowing in the streets. Thirty-Thirty Martinue, red-eyed with Joe Gideon whisky, was reeling down the board sidewalks with a smoking six-gun in each hand. Every few feet he would pause, reel, and blast at a sign or watering trough and roar with anguish.

"Sold th' land!" he swore. "Raised 'im from a pup. Worked myself to the grave for him. And he sold th' land—" He started crying, screwing up his seamed, weather-beaten face. He wiped a forearm across his eyes. Then the focal point of his rage would return to him and he'd let out another howl of fury. "Sold it to that no-good varmint sheepherder, Zepeda—all on account of that cheap, furrin' French woman he married!" He blasted at a hitch rail.

In the Cherokee Flats hotel Red Martinue awoke to the ruckus in the street below. He turned and looked at the tousled head of his beautiful wife, Celeste, on the pillow beside his. Her fingers were curled against her flushed cheeks and she was sleeping with a smile on her lips, undisturbed by the noise in the street. Red knew that however Thirty-Thirty felt, she was worth anything he'd done.

He slipped out of bed. From his window he looked down at the reeling, cussing man in the street. He swore softly and got into his clothes.

By the time Red got down to the street, the sheriff was there, arguing with Thirty-Thirty. When the old brush popper saw his son, he shoved the lawman aside. He stood there reeling, his eyes small and red with fury, a smoking six-gun in each hand. "I orta shoot you," he whispered. "I swear that's whut I orta do—"

Red faced the old man. "Go ahead, Pa," he said gently. "Reckon I'm too old to spank now—"

Old Thirty-Thirty Martinue stood there, a man stiff from forty years in the saddle, knotted and lumped from the beating and thorning the monte had given him, silver-haired from the years and leather-hided from the elements. He stood there while the visions that had driven and sustained him crumpled and faded from his eyes and he became old. "All for a woman," he breathed. "A no-count, easy, black-headed wench—"

The old man laughed. It was a bitter, dry sound, like the parched rustling of prairie grass in a bad drought. He turned, shoved the sheriff out of his path and walked to where his horse was tied. He moved slowly, dragging his feet. "Sold the land—" he whispered to himself, over and over, as if testing the words for their credibility.

CHAPTER SIXTEEN

"A beautiful woman," Manuel Vera began, "is like the monte."

He paused to sip again at the small glass of tequila in his right hand. There was a way a man drank tequila properly. He held the small glass of clear liquid in his right hand and drank it, bringing it carefully to his lips as if it were full and there was a bead rimming the glass. Then he placed it on the table and with the right hand picked up the slice of lemon from the saucer and bit into it. A lick, then, at the salt that had been sprinkled on the back of his left hand, and it was done. And the warmth spread through his belly into his blood and eased his mind and filled his heart with a wisdom and philosophy denied a sober man.

Manuel drank the tequila in a small adobe cantina on the edge of Cherokee Flats where the *vaqueros* came on Saturday nights, and he discussed this matter with a young cousin who had recently become a naturalized Texas citizen by swimming across the Rio Grande on horseback when nobody was looking.

"A beautiful woman is like the monte," Manuel repeated. "She has a beauty like the *lluvia-de-oro*, the shower of gold tree, but there are thorns hidden in her softness. She can be sweet like the *vara dulce*, but she can stab you to death. You can find good in her or evil, whichever you search for, since they are both there. But her ways are full of mystery and there are pitfalls for a man who tries to know her.

"For many years I rode for the Lazy R, for the old *patrón* and the young *patrón*. That old *patrón*—I tell you, he was *muy hombre*. Beyond a doubt you have heard the story of the men of Cortina, the *ladinos* who he branded with the hot iron like cows. And the young *patrón*, he was *muy bravo*. When these *ladinos*, hired by the evil ones of the Boxed X ranch came to our rancho with guns and fire, the young *patrón* ran out and single-handed killed more than a dozen, so—and so—"

He briefly acted out the event, ducking behind tables and chairs and firing at imaginary invaders with his cocked fingers. Men came from the bar with drinks in their hands to listen, because Manuel's reputation as a storyteller was known the length and breadth of the *brasada*.

Manuel picked off his even dozen of the imaginary Boxed X invaders, and then, slightly winded from the feat, returned to his table and refreshed himself from his glass of tequila. He sipped, bit the lemon, licked the salt, and wiped the back of his hand across his lips, shaking his head sadly. "But now the days of the old *patrón* and the young *patrón* and the ranch of the Lazy R have ended. We drove the cattle to Dodge City—ah, such a herd that you couldn't believe, stretching as far as the eye could see and taking many hours to pass a given point. Those were the days they paid in gold for cattle, so much gold that each man, even the lowliest *vaquero*, was given a sack full of it that he could hardly lift when we came to the end of the trail in Dodge City.

"It was at this time, at this city of Dodge, when the young *patrón* met this beautiful woman. Her beauty was such that no man could describe it. Her voice was like the song of mockingbirds in the summer night. Her eyes were soft and dark, like the dove's. She had fair skin such as no woman you have seen from this land. Chihuahua, a man could dream of this for the rest of his days.

"The young *patrón* brought this woman back. But her husband, an evil one filled with bad spirits and *loco* in the head, came here to Cherokee Flats to kill them both. But the young *patrón* threw himself in the path of the bullets to save the beautiful young *señora* that he loved, stopping a half-dozen bullets or more with his body. No man could have stood on his feet so mortally wounded, but the young *patrón* had the strength of ten men and the love of the beautiful young *señora* in his heart, and he pulled his gun and shot the evil one right between the eyes, killing him with a single bullet."

Manuel paused for dramatic effect while he had another sip of tequila, bite of lemon, and lick of salt. "The doctor said that no man could live so badly wounded, but the beautiful young *señora* prayed over the young *patrón* for six days and six nights, going without sleep or food, and at last the Holy Mother heard her prayers and spared the young *patrón* and he became well again and they were married."

Here Manuel's face grew sad and he sighed, shaking his head. "But the story ends very sadly because of the evil spirits in a woman of such unearthly beauty. The young *patrón* became as a man drugged by her beauty. He was *muy borracho*, drunk with his love for her, so that she put her spell on him, and he sold his share of the great Lazy R ranch to the evil ones of the Boxed X. He did this forgetting everything, even his own father, the old *patrón*, so that he could give the beautiful woman many fine things of gold and silver.

"Now they live in town and the young *patrón* has become a businessman and he no longer rides the monte and he is no longer *muy hombre* in the old ways. He is sick in his soul with this woman. He is like a man sick with the craving for marijuana that he must have every day or die.

"He has invested his money wisely and it is said he is very prosperous now. The beautiful *señora* wears gowns from New Orleans that cost more than a man could make from riding in the brush for a year. He owns an overland freight company and a packery on the coast. And they have bought the old Red Lantern saloon where the young *patrón* was born many years ago and made it very fine. You can go and see for your-self that there is no saloon to compare with it anywhere between San Antonio and Brownsville.

"The young *patrón* wears a fine business suit and

there is an office you must go to if you wish to speak to him, where he keeps the money and books on his business. But it is whispered that the young *señora* is the true *patrón* of the business. Under the softness of such a woman there is a strength and ruthlessness a man does not suspect.

"The old *patrón* just sits forgotten in his ranch house, too drunk to ride in the saddle any more. I stay with him, to see to the few horses that are left, and to sell a few skins. But there is no more money, hardly enough for this tequila I drink on Saturday night. The old *patrón* will soon die of *sentimiento*, I think—of a broken heart."

Manuel finished his tequila. "You see, it is as I told you—a beautiful woman is like the monte."

As the time passed, Celeste had taken over most of the running of their business in Cherokee Flats, managing the saloon and the freight office, while Red traveled each week to the freight office in Corpus Christi and the packery on the Gulf coast. He had been surprised at what a cool business head she had on her pretty shoulders. But then, as she had once warned him—he really hadn't known her very well.

A great number of packeries were in operation along the Texas coast in the early 1870s during the years that the price of beef hit rock bottom and there was more money in hides and tallow. There wasn't a great deal of cost involved. Some barrels of salt, a slaughter pen, vats, ropes, pulleys, butcher knives, and a shed or two, and a man was in business.

The hides were taken off the animals and some of the beef was salted and pickled, but most of it was rendered and after the tallow was cooked from the meat it was dumped into the bay or fed to the hogs. Since the loin contained no tallow it was thrown away or given to anyone who wanted it. You could have a wagonload of choice loin steaks for the asking.

The dead carcasses of cattle were piled high until acres of them surrounded a packery, fouling the air for miles and drawing clouds of buzzards. Red loathed the business. But there was money in it. In 1874, one hundred and two million pounds of tallow and $2,560,000 worth of hides were exported from the United States.

Once, while Red was at the packery, rifle shots crashed through the shed roof. Red ran to the door of the shed.

A lone rider was outlined against the sky on a nearby hummock. He was slouched over in his saddle, a smoking rifle in his arms. His eyes burned like twin coals from the dark shadows of his hat, as he glared at the acres of bloated carcasses around him.

"Had to come see how low a cowman could sink!" he yelled. He took a pull at a half-empty bottle of Joe Gideon whisky that had been stuck under his shirt, and reeled in his saddle. "Dead cow business!" he snorted. "Hell, you ain't a man no more. You're a stinkin' buzzard! Smelt you clear up to th' Nueces." He tilted the bottle again, drained it and threw it at the shed.

Then he turned, slumped and reeling in the saddle,

and rode back toward the brush, letting his horse pick his way between the carcasses, stirring up the swarms of buzzards that had settled on the dead cattle.

Red watched Thirty-Thirty disappear into the brush, riding back where the air smelled of the retama blossom instead of dead cows, and the mockingbird sang in the thickets at night. And then Red got a bottle of whisky and got drunk himself.

He had to stay drunk the whole time he was down at the packery to bear the stench and blood and flies and buzzards. And when he rode back to Cherokee Flats, he burned the clothes he had worn, and soaked in a barbershop bathtub for an hour before he would go near his house.

But that night he watched Celeste brush her hair until it snapped, and then undress, letting the yellow lamplight fall on the smooth curves and shadows of her whiteness and then come to him with fire in her lips and hunger in her loins. And everything was blotted from his mind except the obsession for her that burned all the will power from him.

They were making good money from the packing shed and the overland freight wagons and the saloon, but in order to forget how he hated the business he was in and longed for the freedom of the range, Red drank too much.

He came home to the fine house they had bought, his tongue thick with liquor, and he talked about going back to ranching. "Beef is bringin' a price again," he said. "There's talk of makin' cattle drives to Kansas again next spring. All the ranches are startin' to round up herds again and brand them 'stead of skinnin' them.'"

But she replied in a low, firm voice. "I'll never go back to live in that godforsaken brush. We're doing so well now. We'd be fools to go back to the gamble of ranching."

"There's more to life than makin' money," Red said, his tongue thick and his head spinning from the liquor he'd drunk.

She shook her head. "That's the most important thing. Nothing else is any good without it. I was poor when I lived with my father, and poor when Leslie lost his plantation, and poor the first year you and I were married, living out in the brush. Remember this, Red," she said through her teeth, "I'll never be poor again! I tried to tell you when you wanted to marry me. I tried to tell you there was another person inside me that I couldn't fight. A person that could be selfish and greedy. Well, that person has taken over and I like it just fine. For the first time in my life I'm beginning to have what I want."

"They say that the dealers you're hirin' for the gamblin' tables at the Red Lantern saloon are crooked—"

"We're in business," she said coolly. "Our dealers have to show a good percentage for the house. How they do it is their business."

"So we cheat people who have been my friends and neighbors all my life," Red said bitterly. "And what if I told you I was goin' to sell out this stinkin', crooked business we're in an' go back to ranching, anyway?"

"Then, Red," she said quietly, "I'd say you'd go back without me." And there was a steadiness in her eyes that warned him that the words were no bluff.

He left the house to drink some more. But that solved little, because his need for her was too great, burning in him like the need for a drug. And he had to go back to her soft arms and lips, which could carry him beyond thinking.

He tried to see Thirty-Thirty. But when he walked up to him on the street, the old man turned his back and strode away. And once Red rode out to the ranch and Thirty-Thirty came out on the porch with a rifle in his hand and a bullet howled past Red's ear. "You're trespassin' on my land," he said coldly. "I got no more son—"

Red turned his horse and rode back to town to the woman who was now all he had.

CHAPTER SEVENTEEN

It was true that the beef markets in Kansas had opened again and once more there was a need and a price for Texas cattle. There were cattle drives the spring of 1875 and the ranchers and *vaqueros* came back with their pockets full. They poured into the New Red Lantern saloon when they got back to Cherokee Flats, with plenty of money to spend. And Celeste found it profitable to remodel the saloon and enlarge it. She had carpenters knock out a wall, doubling the size of the gambling casino and building a stage at one end for the entertainment she was planning to provide. These men who came back from Dodge City had seen the glitter of big things. Now, unless they could find the likes of it in Cherokee Flats, they'd go to San Antonio or Matamores to spend their money. Celeste intended to see to it that their money stayed in Cherokee Flats, more specifically in the cash registers of the New Red Lantern.

She bought an elegant mahogany Brunswicke-Balke-Collander bar and backbar with a mirror that stretched the length of one wall. She made a special trip to New Orleans, where she bought a sparkling glass chandelier so large a single freight wagon was filled with it, bringing it overland from the nearest port of Corpus Christi. She bought pool tables, cues, and poker chips, all with a miniature red lantern stamped on them. And while she was in New Orleans, she hired a troupe of dancing girls.

The night the New Red Lantern opened after the remodeling, it was ablaze with light and rocking with music from a five-piece Mexican orchestra. Each customer was welcomed with a beer stein full of champagne and a free one-dollar poker chip to start him at the gaming tables.

They came from far and wide, ranchers and gamblers, wide-eyed cowmen from the brush country and fresh off the trail coming home from Dodge City. They gawked at the enormous chandelier, scattering chips of light around the room like diamonds from its thousands of facets of tinkling glass.

And when the footlights went on at the stage and the orchestra gave a fanfare, they stared avidly at the beautiful girls who danced wickedly, showing stockinged legs and garters.

Celeste, herself, appeared on the opening night program. She was dressed in a low-cut evening gown she had brought back from New Orleans. The *décolleté* top of the dress bared a generous curve of bosom marked by a black beauty patch. Red was out of the city that night, at Corpus Christi to see about business at the other end of their freight line. He would not have allowed her to appear in public dressed like that.

She sang heart-rending ballads like "Lorena" and "The Dying Cowboy," and tears ran freely down the leathery cheeks of hard-bitten cowmen. And she sang stirring war songs, "The Yellow Rose of Texas" and "Dixie," and the men stomped and whistled and fired their guns at the ceiling.

Duncan Zepeda had ridden into town that night. He stood at the bar in the New Red Lantern with a drink in his hands and his eyes stared at Celeste hungrily. He had not forgotten that first time he'd seen her, the day his father bought Red's half of the Lazy R. He had bided his time, knowing that in time he would have her. And now, seeing her like this tonight, he knew that he was through waiting.

The next day he was in a barbershop getting a shave when he saw her walk past the window on her way to the freight office.

"That wife of Red Martinue," he said. "Sure is a good-lookin' woman."

"Oh, she's a looker all right," the barber winked.

"Seen her last night singin' at the Red Lantern," Duncan went on. "Don't reckon she's much of a respectable woman, showin' herself in a saloon that-a-way."

"Can't tell about that. They say she was a stage actress when Red found her. You know how them stage actresses are. They'll go right into a saloon with men and not think nothin' of it."

"I hear Red's away from town a whole lot of the time these days with his freighting business," Duncan said. "Must get kinda hard on a red-blooded woman like that, doin' without her husband so much of the time."

The men in the barber shop all laughed at that.

"Don't reckon any feller's helpin' her out while Red's away?"

"Oh, I couldn't say about that," the barber said. "That Red's a hot-blooded young buck. He killed the first man she was married to, you know. Shot him down right over there in front of the livery stable. I reckon a feller'd think twice 'fore he went to messin' 'round with any woman of Red Martinue's."

"Some fellers, maybe," Duncan said, "if they was scared of Red. But you know somethin', I ain't scared of Red Martinue even a little bit."

The barber finished the shave, wiping the soap out of Duncan's ears with his towel, and dusting his face with talcum powder. Duncan got out of the chair, flipped a coin at the barber, and got his Stetson from a peg on the wall.

"Gonna stop by an' say howdy to Mizz Martinue, Duncan?" one of the men sitting on the bench in the shop asked. The other men all laughed and nudged one another in the ribs.

"Might just do that," Duncan said, grinning.

He sauntered down the boardwalk until he came to the building with a sign out front that bore the lettering: MARTINUE FREIGHT OFFICE. He studied the sign for a moment, then opened the door and walked in.

Celeste was alone in the office. She looked up from her books. When she saw who had entered, her eyes narrowed. "Yes?" she asked coolly.

"Mornin', Mizz Martinue," Duncan Zepeda said in a soft voice, moving up to the desk.

"Was there something you wanted?"

"I reckon," he grinned, looking at her. Then he said, "Nice mornin', ain't it? Hot yesterday, but I reckon it'll cool a little today."

Her eyes were narrow and chilly. "Did you want to have some freight shipped, Mr. Zepeda?"

"That's about the size of it." He smiled. He placed his hands palms down on the desk and rested his weight on them, leaning over the desk. "I was at the Red Lantern last night. Heard you sing. Never heard anything so pretty."

"Thank you," she said in a cool, brisk voice. She closed her books and stood up. "Now what was it you wanted to ship?"

He sat on the edge of the desk, his eyes slowly traveling down her figure. "You sure looked nice last night, Mizz Martinue," he said softly. "I never seen a dress quite like that one you had on." His eyes came to rest on her bosom and he chuckled. "That was some dress, all right."

She blushed to the roots of her hair. The way he was looking at her she felt like she didn't have a stitch of clothes on this minute. "Mr. Zepeda," she said angrily, "I'm too busy to pass the time of day. If you have some freighting business, please tell me what it is or get out!"

His lips pursed. "Don't pay to be in such an all-fired rush, Mizz Martinue. I figured to be sociable a while first. No reason why we can't be friends now, is there?"

"There's every reason," she whispered, trembling with anger. "Now get out of this office!"

His eyes drank her in. "Lord, you're a beautiful woman when you're mad like that," he said thickly. He moved from the corner of the desk, around to where she was standing. She shrank back, against a wall, and he stood inches from her.

She was shaking with indignation. "You're either drunk or crazy!"

"Both," he said softly. "Drunk and crazy both. Drunk and crazy wantin' you. Ever since that day in the hotel room. You know it. You saw it then. A woman sees it in a man—"

Her hand went to her throat. "Listen, Red will kill you," she gasped. "If I tell him you came in here and insulted me with that kind of talk, he'll go after you with a gun!"

Duncan Zepeda's gloved hand slowly moved up to his cheek and he rubbed the scar there while his eyes burned on her. "Yeah, you tell him about this," he murmured. "You tell him everything that happened today. Red and I are long overdue. You understand? You tell him, see, because I'm gettin' sick of having him in this town. You tell him I came here while he was gone and I talked to you like this, you hear? You tell him I looked at you in the hotel room that day and I wanted you. I've been wanting you since that first minute. You tell your husband Red Martinue that so's he'll come after me with a gun and we can get this thing between us settled and done with, because I'm sick of him even livin' in the same state with me."

Sweat was standing out across his face and his eyes were fixed and he was trembling with the tension and fury of the hate that washed through him. He caught her arms, holding her roughly. "When we were kids I beat him and took his knife away from him. When we grew up I took his half of the Lazy R ranch away from him. And now I'm going to take his woman. And you just tell him that—"

His mouth smashed down on hers. She struggled, fighting and twisting against him, but he was a strong man. She tried to cry out, but his mouth was on hers, muffling her voice. He kissed her hungrily. Then he looked down at her, panting. "You fight me," he said. "Every time I come for you, you fight me like this. Dig your claws in me and bite like a wildcat. Show me just how much of a woman you are, because that puts the fire in a man's blood. This is enough for now. But I'll be back." He turned and strode out of the office.

She fell into the office chair, sobbing hysterically. She held the front of her torn dress together and scrubbed the back of her hand across her mouth. "Oh my God—" she screamed.

Finally she pulled herself together enough to stumble to the back room for a pitcher of water. She poured it over her face and hands and washed her bruised lips until they felt raw. Then she sank into a chair, sick at the stomach and trembling, and tried to think. If she told Red when he came home, he would strap on his gun and go after Duncan Zepeda as certainly as the sun rose over the monte every morning. There would be a killing, Duncan or Red, or both. But if she didn't tell him— The parting words of Duncan Zepeda echoed in her ears: "I'll be back and the next time I'll have more—"

CHAPTER EIGHTEEN

Red Martinue returned to Cherokee Flats at the end of the week, and when he walked into the office, a rancher, Raymond Spann, a man he had known for many years was waiting to see him. "It's—well, it's kinda personal, Red. It's about your pa, Thirty-Thirty. Reckon we could go someplace where we could have a drink and talk?"

Red was tired and dusty after the long ride from Corpus Christi, but he nodded. "Sure, Raymond. Let's go over to the saloon."

There wasn't much business this time of day. Red's throat was parched from the heat and dust of the road. He ordered a big glass of cold tap beer.

Spann turned his glass of whisky around on the table self-consciously, making little wet rings. "This is pretty hard to say, Red. I don't mean to make no trouble. I hope you'll take it in the right way. I've known Thirty-Thirty most of my life. I've drunk with him, played poker with him since we came to Texas more 'n thirty years ago. I—well, I know about the trouble you and him's had since you sold out your half of the Lazy R two years ago. He's been drinkin' awful heavy since then, Red, and gamblin'. I guess you and that ranch was all he ever lived for and now he just don't give a hang. We got in a poker game in Laredo last week. Hell of a game. Went on for three days. Thirty-Thirty'd used up the last of his money. He—well, he put up his remaining half of the Lazy R in the game, Red." He swallowed the whisky in a single gulp and wiped the back of his hand across his mouth. He took out a bundle of scribbled I.O.U.'s from his pocket. "I won the game. He give me these I.O.U.'s and asked for a week to cover them before I went down and registered the deeds to his land in my name."

Spann sighed, shaking his head. "I swear, I'd rather take a beating than take that ranch away from Thirty-Thirty. It's goin' to kill the old man. But I know he won't never be able to raise the money in a week and there's nothin' I can do. I ain't so rich I can afford to throw all of this away. Beef's goin' up every day. It's worth too much to sell the skin off cows any more, and everybody thinks it'll keep goin' up. That place of Thirty-Thirty's will be worth somethin' in a few years, even if you did sell off half to Zepeda. Besides, you know Thirty-Thirty. He ain't takin' charity off no man. Stiff-necked and proud as he is, a gamblin' debt is like his word of honor. Why, if I tried to give the deeds back to him, he'd come after me with a gun."

Red listened with a growing tightness in his chest. "Thank you for comin' to me about this, Raymond," he said quietly.

"Hell, it was the only thing I could figure to do. I said

to my wife just last night, Tm goin' to Red Martinue about this.' You're his son, Red. He might take help off you where he wouldn't off any other man. I figured I'd tell you about this. If you want to buy the I.O.U.'s off me, well all right. If you don't, that's your business, but leastways, I'll ease my mind because I gave you the chance."

Red nodded. "I appreciate that, Raymond. I'll buy those I.O.U.'s. You'll have to give me a few days. I got the money in the bank to cover part of it. I can get that to you right away for a down payment. I'll have to sell my business. That will cover most of the rest. If there's some left, I'll give you a note for it, and we'll round up a herd from Thirty-Thirty's land and sell them for the balance. I hear beef's bringin' a good price in Kansas now."

"Hell, that's fair enough." Spann warmly shook hands with Red. "I don't mind tellin' you I'd a-liked to have got my hands on that place of Thirty-Thirty's, but I feel a site better in my conscience about settling it this way."

Spann left and Red sat alone at the table, switching from beer to straight whisky. His body was gritty and sticky with sweat from the long hot ride. He was tired and his heart was heavy because he knew he had come to the end of the line with Celeste. It wasn't so much of a matter of choosing between her and Thirty-Thirty as it was a matter of choosing at last whether he could still be a man and live with himself, or not be a man.

He went home and he told Celeste what he had to do.

"I know how you feel about stayin' in business. We've talked about it before. I know what you said you'd do if I went back to the ranch. But I can't do any different, Celeste. I've already sold Thirty-Thirty down the river till he don't care if he lives or dies. I can't put the last bullet in his back. I'm going to sell out. The packery, the freighting company, the house, everything. I'm goin' to pay off the I.O.U.'s on his place and go back and help him get a herd together again."

Celeste listened, her face stiff and white, her hands clenched. "You mean you'd throw away everything we worked so hard for these past two years!" she cried. "You'd sell a good business just to pay off an old man's gambling debts? You'd go back to the hell-hole in the brush, breaking your back, working your heart out in the heat and the thorns—"

He shook his head. "It's more than just payin' off the gamblin' debts, Celeste. I guess we've both known in our hearts this time had to come one day. I'm a rancher. I'll never be anythin' else. A man has to do the work that his heart tells him to do or he's not a man any more. I'm sorry."

"Then I'm sorry too," she whispered. "Because I'm not going back there with you, Red. It'll be the end of our marriage."

There was a hurting in Red's throat and a blinding in his eyes. He looked at the beautiful woman he prized more than all his other possessions on earth, more than his own life, and a knife twisted in his heart. But he knew he couldn't go on loving her if he couldn't love himself.

"I'll leave you the saloon. I won't sell that," he promised her. "You're makin' good money with it. You can sell it if you like, or keep running it, That's up to you."

He looked at her one more time, memorizing every precious line of her face. Then he turned and left the house.

Celeste stood there, trembling with frustration. She stamped her foot. "Oh, what a stubborn fool he is!" she cried. Then she dissolved into tears.

He rode out to the Lazy R. When Thirty-Thirty heard his horse in the yard he came reeling out to the porch. He was tanked to his bristling eyebrows with Joe Gideon whisky. He stared at Red and yelled, "Git off my propitty!" He drew his six-gun and lead howled past Red's ear.

Red swung off the horse. A bullet plowed into the dust at his feet. He spun his reins around the gnarled hitch rail. Another bullet sang over his head.

"You never could shoot worth a dang, you crazy old coot!" he yelled at Thirty-Thirty. "But I'd sure feel easier about it if you'd stop because you're so dang drunk you might hit me by accident!"

Manuel Vera ran around the corner of the barn to see what all the shooting and yelling was about. "*Señor* Red!" he cried excitedly.

"See if you can get that ornery old buzzard on the porch to stop using me for target practice," Red yelled to the foreman. "I came all the way out here to help him get his fool ranch out of the fire."

Manuel and Red scouted around and hired back some of their old hands, loyal enough to work for half-wages with a promised bonus when they reached Kansas with the trail herd.

They worked the brush day and night. Red was soft from his two years as a businessman and he got too stiff to move. He worked without sleep, sometimes dozing in the saddle. The last days of gathering the herd were feverish, filled with the bawling of cattle, the smell of the branding iron singeing hair, the clatter of horns, shout of men, creaking of saddle leather and the everlasting heat and dust.

Thirty-Thirty stayed in the ranch house drunk on Joe Gideon whisky and sulked. But on that last morning, when the herd was strung out and starting north, he came out on the ranch porch, red-eyed and trembling, but sober. He was buckling on his gun belt and pulling down his hat-brim. He went up to Red's horse and laid a gnarled and thorn-knotted hand on the saddle horn. "Son," he said, "I'd sure admire to ride along on this drive up to Dodge."

Red smiled down at the silver-haired old man, his horse pawing and stirring restlessly in the dust under him, and peace came between the two men.

The venerable brush popper was so stiff from his year-long drunk that they had to lift him creaking in every joint and groaning into his saddle. But once he was aboard and moving, he sweated all the alcohol out of his system and limbered up. And before the drive was over, he was outworking, outriding, and outcussing the youngest hand in the bunch.

They drove up to the rail head in Kansas, across the rolling prairie, through the dust and the sage and the tumbleweeds, across the rivers and between the canyons. They sneaked through hostile Indian country, sweated out thunderstorms that boogered the cattle, broke up stampedes and coaxed stubborn longhorns into wading rivers. They made it up to Kansas, sweat-stained and dust-coated and they sold the herd for enough money to pay off the balance of the I.O.U.'s and put the Lazy R solidly back into the cattle business, half-sized though it now was.

But at the time they were starting back to Texas Duncan Zepeda sat at a table in the Red Lantern saloon, talking to a man who rode for him. "I want you to head out for Kansas. If you stick to the regular cow trails, you'll meet the Lazy R crew on the way back. They must be leaving Dodge about now, so you'll probably find them halfway. When you do, give this message to Red Martinue. Tell him I've taken his woman. If he comes back to this town again, I'll be waiting for him with a gun."

CHAPTER NINETEEN

The men of the Lazy R rode into Cherokee Flats and the dust curled from beneath the hooves of their horses and drifted into the early morning air. They rode into the main street in a body. The men and women who saw them left the streets and went to their homes. They knew of the trouble between the Martinues and the Zepedas and they knew there would be blood in the streets of Cherokee Flats today.

The Lazy R riders stopped at the first saloon near the end of the street, tied their horses at the hitch rails and stood rolling cigarettes and looking up and down the quiet street.

Red bent down and tied the leather thong of his gun holster more tightly around his thigh. He lifted the gun from the oiled holster and dropped it back, testing it to see that it was free and slipped out easily in the hand. His eyes were flat and for the moment he moved in a detached manner without the pull and current of emotion.

Thirty-Thirty bit off a chew of tobacco. "I guess I'll go in the saloon. Maybe they have to ride in from the ranch."

"No, I reckon they're in town now. He'd have scouts ride in to tell him we reached Cherokee Flats."

But Red went in the saloon with Thirty-Thirty and ordered a glass of whisky. The liquor burned his stomach this early in the morning, but it steadied his hand.

He heard the quick tap of heels on the board sidewalk outside. The batwings opened. Celeste stood there, just inside the saloon, her eyes adjusting to the cool darkness inside the room. She stared at Red across the room, her eyes wide and stained dark in her frightened face.

Red felt the pull and surge of emotion start up in him. He had tried to push it away until after the business at hand, because an emotion-driven man was not a good man with a gun. But she had heard the wildfire news racing up the street that the Martinues were back from Dodge City and she had come running to see him. Now he looked at her and the emotion boiled in him, making his hands tremble.

The words of the man Duncan Zepeda had sent after him burned across his mind like the smoking wound of a hot branding iron. "Tell Red Martinue that I've taken his woman—"

He looked across the room at Celeste, his wife. But she was no longer Celeste-His-Wife. Now she was another man's woman. It was impossible to say that he no longer loved her. Emotion was a raging torrent in him, hate and jealousy and bitterness and fury. He looked at his woman, realizing with a sickness in his stomach that now her beauty was for another man, a hated man. And a wave of feeling rose in him so great that it blinded him. His hand closed unconsciously around the whisky glass in his hand until the glass broke and blood spilled between his clenched fingers. But he was aware of no physical pain because the other pain was too great.

She came toward him slowly, across the room, her tear-filled eyes fixed on him. "Red, I know what he told you," she whispered. "He told me the message he was sending you. It isn't true. Red, I swear to God in heaven it isn't true. He's tried—" She swallowed hard. "Ever since you went to Dodge, he has been after me, fighting me, trying to beat me down, driving me out of my mind." She shook her head. "I swear he never succeeded. He sent you that message because he wanted a gunfight with you. He wants to kill you so he can keep on after me until he gets what he wants."

She put her hands on his broad chest. Her eyes were brimming with tears. "I love you, Red," she whispered. "I was wrong—about everything. I didn't know anyone could feel such pain and loneliness in their heart. I want you back—on any terms. I'll be anything you ask, a ranch wife, anything—"

Slowly, his hands moved up and he cupped her face and he looked into her eyes. His heart believed her words and filled with a joy that choked him. "Celeste—" he whispered shakily.

Tears spilled from her eyes. "Can you ever forgive me, *mon chéri*? It was that other girl in me—the bad one I told you about that my mother put there, but she'll never come back again, I promise!" She turned her tear-wet face into his hands, kissing his palms.

Then she looked up at him again, the fright coming back into her face, and she pleaded, "We have to ride away. Now, before Duncan comes. He's in town, at the hotel with his men, waiting for you." She seized his hand. "Please, we can ride away now, fast, before there's any trouble—"

He squeezed her hand. "I'm afraid it's too late for that, Celeste. This thing has to be settled."

"*Señor* Red!" Manuel called from the boardwalk outside.

Red went to the batwings. He saw Duncan Zepeda come out of the hotel down the street. He walked out into the street, smoking a cigarette, looking down at the Lazy R horses. He crossed the street and stood in the shadow of the walk and threw his cigarette away.

Red moved out to the sidewalk and Thirty-Thirty followed him, carrying one of the new Winchester Model 73 repeating rifles that he'd bought in Dodge City.

The *vaqueros* of the Lazy R moved away from their horses, toward the shelter of the boardwalks on either side of the street. Then there was a sudden puff of smoke from a rooftop and the crack of a rifle and one of the *vaqueros* in the street spun around and sprawled in the dust.

Thirty-Thirty threw the Winchester to his shoulder, firing rapidly, working the lever, but he couldn't be sure that he'd hit the sniper.

In the bank building at the center of the street Josiah Zepeda put down his cigar and finished signing some papers on his desk. He opened a drawer and took out a brace of six guns in oiled leather holsters. He turned and nodded to the two big men in his office. They looked at one another, sweat glistening on their faces. But they moved together to pick up his chair and they carried it out of the front door and sat him down at the edge of the walk.

He leaned back in his chair, savoring his cigar, turning it between his teeth, forgetting for a moment the wracking pain in his body as he studied the situation in the street. Then he drew one of the six guns and swung it up, getting a quick bead on one of the Lazy R men. He fired and the man spilled forward, clutching at a post on the boardwalk. Zepeda grunted with satisfaction. He fired again, missing with this shot, but following it with another quick one that spun a man out from behind a water barrel.

Manuel Vera fired at Josiah Zepeda, splintering the arm of his chair. Then the gun spilled from the Lazy R foreman's hand and he spun around, clutching his bleeding shoulder.

Thirty-Thirty swore. "Old bastid ain't lost his gun eye." He threw down on Zepeda with the Winchester and fired rapidly.

In his chair Josiah Zepeda jerked upright, dropping his gun. He reached for his cigar, but it tumbled out of his mouth. He was smiling as he slid out of the chair and rolled over in the dust of the street at the edge of the boardwalk. The sun was in his eyes, but it could not bother him, and the pain that had wracked his body for three long years was over.

From the other side of the street Duncan yelled "Pa!" in an anguished voice. Then he ran out to the middle of the street. "You killed him. You killed my pa!" he sobbed.

Red moved from the shelter of the saloon doorway out into the street. "You started this trouble, Duncan," he called out. "You got your pa killed."

Duncan wiped the angry tears from his eyes with the back of his hand. He began walking toward Red Martinue, walking down the dead center of the street with his hand moving toward his gun, ignoring everything else except the man in front of him, and a dead silence fell over the street, and the other men on both sides held their gunfire.

"I kin pick him off from here easy," Thirty-Thirty called, clutching the Winchester.

But Red was standing out in the street and he said, "Stay back, Pa. This is between us."

He had a fleeting glimpse out of the corner of his eye of Celeste's white face at the saloon doorway, and then he walked to meet Duncan.

He felt the heat of the sun on his head and hot on the dust at his feet. It simmered over the street and the roofs and stung his eyes. The street narrowed down to a tunnel filled at the far point by the figure of the man coming toward him. Red watched Duncan's hand move up and rub the scar on his cheek as he walked in measured steps. Then Duncan's hand moved in a lightning flash for his gun.

Red stopped, spraddle-legged, and his gun was in his hand and he fired, half-crouched, seeing the other man's gun blaze and feeling the slap of lead close to his cheek.

Duncan Zepeda stared at him. He looked around at the men on either side of the street. Then he turned and began walking away in jerking steps. He dropped his gun and spread his hands over his chest, trying to hold back the blood, but it spurted between his fingers. Then his knees buckled and he sprawled out in the dust.

It took them a few days to get all of Celeste's things moved out to the ranch house and arranged the way she wanted them. She had fine furniture now, a grand piano and a sideboard of deep rich mahogany and a set of cut-glass. And there were two wardrobes full of dresses.

"This house!" she pouted. "Red, you have to promise to build me a new one right away, one twice as big and fine for my nice furniture, so we can entertain rich people, and—"

"Hey," he laughed. "First, we're goin' to buy back the land from the Zepedas' heirs. Then we'll build a bigger house."

"Humph!" She tossed her head.

He grinned. "You greedy little female. I thought you told me just the other day you'd never be greedy again."

"That was the other day," she said haughtily, "when

I thought you were going to get yourself killed."

He took out a present he had brought back from Dodge City for her, a gold lapel watch studded with diamonds. "Well, I guess there's not much point in givin' you this cheap little ol' thing, then. Might as well just throw it away—"

She stopped pouting and her eyes flew open wide. "Oh, Red, it's beautiful!" she gasped. She pinned it to her dress and pirouetted around the room, watching herself in a mirror. With a lightning change of mood she brimmed with excitement and affection. She sat on his lap and ran her fingers through his hair.

Red shook his head. "I'll never be able to keep up with all the Celestes I married! Now I've got the six-year-old one on my hands."

"Yes, I'm six years old and you're my father," she cried. "So big and strong and fierce!" She kissed him impetuously.

"I don't feel much like a father right now though," Red confessed, putting his hand on her waist.

She looked at him mischievously. She put her warm cheek against his, then kissed him warmly.

But the next instant she was off his lap and running through the house, shrieking every time he came close. Finally, she ran into the bedroom and slammed the door, locking it.

"Celeste, you open that door!" Red thundered.

She giggled on the other side.

"I'll kick it down," he threatened.

"Oh, how fierce!" she cried. "No, I'm afraid o£ you

now. You can't come in." She giggled again.

He rattled the doorknob. Then he heard the key turn softly. He threw the door open and she was standing in the center of the room, breathing hard, her face flushed prettily, her eyes sparkling. She tried to run around him, but he caught her and scooped her up in his big arms and kissed her fiercely.

"Oh!" she gasped. "Are you trying to smother me?" She dug her fingers in his ribs, knowing how ticklish he was. He let her down, laughing helplessly. Then he caught her again and pinned her arms to her sides. "Now!" he cried triumphantly. Then he kissed her until she was breathless.

"Oh, I do love you," she whispered. Her arms crept around him and her eyes grew smoky. They fell silent, lost in a deep kiss.

In the cantina Manuel Vera was holding his young cousin spellbound with his story of the gun battle on the streets of Cherokee Flats. There was a large bandage around his wounded shoulder and he had to favor it when he acted out the crucial points of the battle.

"I tell you, *muchacho,* it was a thing to see. There were dozens of the evil Boxed X men on the rooftops, all firing their guns at me. I ran out into the street and the bullets were like hail around my feet. I picked them off, so and so—" He cocked and fired a deadly forefinger. "They fell off the rooftops like flies with my bullets in them and the street was red with their blood."

He drank the tequila and licked the salt. "And all of this over a beautiful woman." He shook his head. "It is as I told you before. A beautiful woman is like the monte full of strange whims and traps of thorns that are beyond a man to understand!"

One day early the following spring, Thirty-Thirty Martinue came rolling out of a Cherokee Flats saloon, loaded to the teeth with Joe Gideon whisky. He stood in the center of the main street, howling like a Comanche and blasting holes in the sky with his forty-five. Then he set a weaving course for the new county courthouse.

He stumbled into the cattle brands registration office, pushed his bristly countenance across a desk and near asphyxiated the clerk with his whisky breath.

"My name's Thirty-Thirty Martinue," he announced in a voice that shook the windows. "Owner of the Lazy R. Got me a new grandson, borned last night! Spittin' image of me. Done named him Justin. We looked up in th' family Bible and found out that wuz my real name. Named him after his ol' grandpappy, she did! Guess she ain't such a bad woman at that. Now I'm gonna change my brand to the Circle J after my grandson." Thirty-Thirty swaggered. "Me 'n my grandson's gonna build th' Circle J up an' run th' Boxed X an' all the other ranches in th' *brasada* plumb into the river."

He sent a charge of tobacco juice at a spittoon, missing it by a safe margin of three feet. "Yessir, we're gonna build the Circle J into the biggest danged cattle ranch in the whole state of Texas!"

And they danged near did!

ABOUT THE AUTHOR

CHARLES BECKMAN (the pen name of Charles Boeckman) is a native Texan. He grew up during the Great Depression when there was no money for music lessons. Fortunately, everyone in his family played a musical instrument. Those were the days of the big bands and their sounds were on all the A.M. radio stations. Hearing Bennie Goodman and Artie Shaw, he fell in love with the clarinet. He found a fingering chart for the clarinet and taught himself to play that instrument. To get a job on a big band in those days, a reed man was expected to play both saxophone and clarinet, so he also taught himself to play saxophone. The year he graduated from high school, in 1938, he played his first professional job in a South Texas country dance hall. He continued playing weekend jobs in dance halls all over South Texas until the mid 1940s, when he moved to Corpus Christi, Texas, and played as a sideman in bands in that city. In the 1970s he formed his own New Orleans style Dixieland jazz band, which became quite popular. He still plays in the Texas Jazz Festival every October. In recognition of his many years on the music scene in the area, he was awarded a star in the South

Texas Music Walk of Fame in June of 2009.

While music has been a part of his career, his main occupation has been that of a professional writer. He has had dozens of books and hundreds of short stories published all over the world He uses his music background as setting for many of his mystery stories. He sold his first suspense story to *Detective Tales* in 1945. In 1965, he married Patti Kennelly, a school teacher. With Charles's help, she also became a writer. At this writing, they have been happily married for forty-six years. They have a daughter and two grandchildren. In the 1980s they collaborated on a series of twenty-six Harlequin Romance novels that sold worldwide over two million copies.

More about Charles Beckman's career can be found on his web site,

www.charlesboeckman.com

Lightning Source UK Ltd.
Milton Keynes UK
UKOW042353081112

201882UK00001B/92/P